Mary Tales Omnibus

Mary Tales Collections, Volume 1

Mary Tales

Published by Mary Tales Books, 2017.

MARY TALES OMNIBUS

First edition. August 6, 2017.

ISBN: 979-8230940777

Written by Mary Tales.

Also by Mary Tales

Jiggles
Jiggles and the Test Pilot
Jiggles and the Archaeologists
Jiggles and the Flying Boats

Love By The Book
Love By The Book
Love The Weekend

Mary Tales Collections
Mary Tales Omnibus
Contact Adventures
Contact Adventures 2 - First Timers
Cassie Gets it On
The Adventures of Jiggles

Meet The Gang
Meet The Gang

Table of Contents

Closed Circuit

Marcus Dent poured himself a shot of vodka, turned on the wide-screen television and prepared to watch his lover, Rose, have sex with another man. He used the console at his side to flick through the pictures from the many cameras hidden about her flat. He found the object of her desires in the kitchen, pretending to fix the dishwasher. Marcus recognised him as John. Every couple of months Rose would find a 'problem' with one of her kitchen appliances and call John's repair company. She was such a good customer he would deal with her personally. He thought he was just a bit of rough for some ugly old fart's bored mistress.

John packed away his tools and stopped pretending he was doing anything useful. He dusted off his knees, the only dirt he had picked up, and went looking for his client. He found her in the living room, standing on a deep pile rug wearing only a white silk teddy, her deep red hair loose down to her shoulders. 'I'm finished now Miss Standish.' John still didn't know her first name.

"Very good John. How much do I owe you?"

"Oh, I'll send you an invoice in the mail." As their couplings had progressed, their script had descended to the level of a porn magazine's reader's letter. John didn't notice, he was too busy staring at the way her breasts pushed out the teddy, the material so sheer he could see the nipples rising with excitement.

"Come here John, I'd like to show my appreciation with more than just money." Marcus had switched to another camera, allowing a close up of Rose's face. He knew her well enough to detect the little grimace which indicated she was becoming tired of these lines. She would give this performance her all, she always did, but it would be the last time with John.

The repairman put down his tool bag and stepped onto the rug. Rose guided his hands to her one piece of clothing. He gently pushed the thin straps off her shoulders and the teddy dropped to the floor. The sight of Rose's naked body generated a gasp of appreciation from him. She had firm full breasts, tight half moon buttocks and a flat stomach which tapered down to a trimmed triangle of pubic hair. Rose began unbuttoning his shirt.

Rose pulled John's shirt off and signalled that he should stand still while she did what she wanted to him. He was willing to comply. She got down on her knees and released his belt, then unbuttoned and unzipped his trousers. When these had fallen around his ankles she pulled his boxer shorts down to reveal his erection.

As she ran her fingers up and down John's throbbing dick, Rose glanced at the nearest camera, hidden inside a wall clock. She could imagine Marcus, and others, watching avidly as she performed for them. By now John's knob was big and throbbing, Rose just had to kiss it. She ran her tongue over the end, then along the underside to the balls. John sighed and, despite her orders, stroked her shoulders. She looked up and met his gaze. She had been waiting for this all day and didn't need any more foreplay. She wanted John to fill her now, and lay back and spread her legs to show him this.

John quickly threw off his clothes. Naked, he stood over Rose, staring down and admiring her body. Then she reached down and lazily split the lips of her sex. They glistened and pouted at him. He knelt down and drew her knees up as he prepared to enter her. Rose reached out and stroked the length of his cock, then drew it down to her cunt. She only had to lodge its head at the entrance and he slid easily in, so excited and wet was she.

With John's cock in her to the hilt, Rose wrapped her legs around his waist and urged him on. He responded by nuzzling her neck and pulling slowly out of her until only the head of his dick was still in her. Rose had been waiting for this all day, and knew she was going to come very soon. He slid back in smoothly and it felt as if he had grown larger still. Rose couldn't take this slow teasing any more, she urged John to go faster with pressure from her legs.

Eager to keep up with Rose's desires, John's thrusts became shorter and faster. Raising himself to touch the floor with only his hands and toes he began angled thrusts which pressed harder than normal against her clitoris. Rose relaxed her legs and stretched out in a star, crying out with joy at every thrust. John kissed her breasts. Her back began arching up to meet each thrust. She clasped handfuls of the carpet to hold herself down. A flush spread across the underside of her breasts and John licked at it. This drove her over the edge. She wrapped her arms around him and pulled him into a kiss as the orgasm resonated from her toes all the way up to the roots of her hair.

Marcus knew some of the others would be turning off now, thinking the show was over, they would surf through the other video feeds in search of further titillation. But John was still hard in Rose and she would take advantage of that. She signalled him to pull out. When he had moved away she rolled onto her belly and thrust up her arse. John understood the suggestion instantly. He moved behind her and planted kisses on the globes of her buttocks. Then he gently prised the firm hemispheres apart and ran his tongue around the tight rim of her anus, savouring the taste. As she relaxed, John licked saliva into the dilating hole.

He moved again, and Rose felt his hands holding her arse cheeks open. She buried her face in the carpet and waited. The head of John's knob teased at the outside of Rose's anus, then eased in on its lubrication of her own cunt juice. Rose moaned and clutched at the carpet, about to come again. John pushed as far in as he could, then pulled a short way out, savouring the tightness of Rose's back passage. She tensed her muscles around him and drew an appreciative sigh.

Clasped so tightly, John couldn't build up a fast rhythm. He simply drew out and pushed in with slow, measured thrusts. This drew out beautifully and sensually, until Rose came again and the shudders shook her whole body. John held her waist tight and shot warm fluid deep inside her.

Marcus watched the status board as everyone else logged off Rose's feed. They didn't want to see her sending off the repairman, it didn't merit their attention. When he had gone she sat back on her haunches and stared at the wall clock. "How did I do?"

Marcus pressed the intercom button, a privilege only he was allowed, "Not bad, twenty one point two six attention hours in total."

Rose looked upset, "Not my best. I think I need a new washing machine repairman."

Bicycle Race

It had taken three hours of pedalling to get out of the suburbs and onto a country road. I decided to rest for a while before going down the gravel track through the trees. I had just finished my bottle of water when I heard another bike approaching.

She shot past me and skidded to a halt, disappearing briefly in a cloud of dust. When it settled I got a good look at her. Unlike me, in my cut off jeans and tee shirt, she was dressed properly for cycling. Dark hair spilled out of her helmet. She wore deliciously tight cycling shorts and one of those cutaway athletic tops which kept her breasts from bouncing round but bared her toned stomach. Her mountain bike was newer than mine and better equipped. She grinned and nodded down the track in a way that I took as an invitation to a race.

I tossed the empty water bottle into the bin and mounted up. When I had drawn level with her she glanced across, raised her eyebrows as if questioning whether I really wanted to do this, then set off. She was a long way ahead before I had even pushed down on the pedals. The track curved away to the left as we rode up hill, and I didn't gain an inch on her all the way to the top. Then it levelled off and she looked back to taunt me.

I put a lot of effort into my pedalling along that flat, slightly winding stretch. I cut corners and breathed hard with the effort of turning the pedals in the highest gear. I gained on her until I was only four bike lengths behind. I could see the muscles of her taut arse moving under Lycra and the way it hugged her groin. It spurred me on to try even harder to catch her.

She slowed down as we reached the crest of a drop. I caught her and passed her and carried on speeding up. The bike was bouncing all over the place on ruts and holes and I realised with terror that I was losing control. The track bent to the right, but I knew I was going to go straight on, whatever I tried to do. I pulled hard on the back brake and the wheel locked up. The rear of the bike waggled all over the place and then suddenly flew out from under me. I skidded on my backside across the gravel and off the edge of the track into the trees.

The bike hit a tree but I luckily didn't. I landed on the soft mat of grass and dead leaves of the forest floor, managed to miss a second tree and went into a roll. I must have blacked out, because I swear she was beside me as soon as I stopped rolling. "Are you alright?"

"I think you won the race."

"That's not important. Are you alright?"

"I guess so." She was leaning over me and the end of her hair tickled my face. "I think I scraped my leg." She moved to look for wounds and I could feel warm breath against the crotch of my cut offs.

"I think you did. I'm going to have to take a closer look." Before I could say anything deft fingers had released my belt, popped open the buttons and pulled my shorts down to my knees. I hadn't bothered with boxers in the hot weather, but she didn't seem at all fazed that my dick was suddenly on show. She took it between a pair of those skilful fingers and examined it as it grew to its full size. "I haven't got any plasters," she said, "But I know a way to relieve the pain."

She took her helmet off and a mass of hair tumbled out. It veiled my dick from view as a hot mouth closed around it. She was right, I had completely forgotten about the scrapes and bumps from the accident and the branches I lay on which poked at me. I looked up through the trees and savoured the play of her tongue over the head of my knob.

She released my cock, now slippery with saliva, and sat back on her haunches. She hooked her thumbs under either side of her cutaway top and pulled it over her head in an easy movement. Her breasts were perfect, firm half globes tipped with seashell pink nipples. She shuffled forwards and presented one to my mouth.

While I licked the growing tip of a nipple I ran my fingers around the waistband of her cycling shorts. I couldn't find a fastener, so I pushed them down and found she too was wearing nothing under them. I cupped a firm buttock in each hand then moved one round to reach her pussy from behind and continued pushing at the shorts with the other. She was already sopping wet and rode up and down on my questing finger a few times as I tried to find out how much of a tit I could get in my mouth. Then she pushed at the hand that was struggling with her shorts, "Don't do that, you'll make them baggy."

She stood up, or at least tried to. The low branches meant she actually had to bend almost double, allowing me to reach up and stroke her wet and then her dry breast. She peeled the shorts off her thighs, pushed them down to the ground and stepped out of them. Now she was naked but for her pumps and short white socks. Her bush was darker than the hair on her head and the inside of her pouting pussy was at least as dark as the head of my own knob.

She sat down again and expertly impaled herself right up to the hilt of my dick. It felt so good I just had to mouth "Wow". She lifted her backside until I was almost completely out of her, then lowered herself again very slowly. I thrust up to meet her and she responded by moving faster.

We rolled over onto our sides, then I managed to get above her. We kissed, our tongues fighting with each other, as I hooked a hand under her knees and drew them up to my shoulders. I thrust faster and faster. I was going to come very soon. I managed to hold out until she cried that she was coming, then I pumped sperm deep inside her.

I let her legs drop down to the ground and we lay there panting. But there was another sound above our laboured breathing. Somewhere in the distance there was a vehicle and it was coming along the track towards us. Her bike was lying on its side on the track and mine could be seen from it. We rushed to dress, I was lucky in that I only had to pull up my shorts from around my knees, before the vehicle arrived.

We stepped out of the trees just as a large off roader pulled up beside her bike. We must have been quite flushed, because we got a very strange look from the driver and his passenger. "Are you okay?" asked the driver.

"It's okay. I missed the corner, but I'm not hurt." I told him.

"I've given him a going over and I think he's alright, too." She said from behind me.

"If you're absolutely certain....?"

"Oh, absolutely." I said. The driver nodded, put the off roader in gear and drove away. I pulled my bike out of the trees. The front tyre was flat and the wheel rim bent where it had hit the tree. "How the hell am I going to get home on this."

"I parked the car just up the road from where we met. I've got a bike rack remember?"

"Oh yeah. You drove all the way here?"

"Hey, this was your fantasy. Be glad you got me out of the house on a Sunday."

I kissed her. "Oh I am Abigail dearest. Next week we do your fantasy, okay."

"I can't wait."

Double the Pleasure

They had laid out a sheet on the floor and Sally, stripped naked, stretched out on it. Then Jane had rubbed scented massage oil all over her, taking particular care around her nipples and crotch. Jane had stripped off all her own clothes and used parts of her body to supplement the actions of her hands. She teased Sally's nipples up to peaks with her own breasts, whilst forcing the tension from her neck and shoulders. Then she traced her nipples down Sally's body and across her abdomen, stopping to dip both into her navel. Jane's deep red nipples now stood out hard and sensitive, she moved further down Sally and angled one breast to force a bud into Sally's dripping cunt. Sally came as Jane moved the nipple like a tiny dick up and down her fanny. Jane spread more oil on her hands and resumed the massage.

After the massage Sally was relaxed and limp, only the thought of what was to come kept her awake. Jane went to the corner and pulled over her large shoulder bag, opening it beside the sheet to produce a razor and shaving foam. Jane squirted the foam into the curls above Sally's cunt, then massaged it in to the accompaniment of appreciative moans. Jane was about to make the first sweep with the razor when she realised she had no water to clean it with. She put down the razor and walked through to the kitchen. "I knew we'd forgotten something." sighed Sally. She shifted slightly so Mark could see her pussy lips pouting under the foam. Jane returned with a large bowl filled with warm water. She dipped the razor in it and dribbled the excess water into Sally's navel. When Sally stopped giggling, Jane lowered the razor to her bush.

The pubic hair came off in short swipes, revealing slightly pink skin underneath, then Jane would clean the blade in the bowl. Sally controlled her breathing only because she was scared of being cut. Mark moved closer for a better look as Jane made the final swipe. She took an edge of the sheet and dabbed it over Sally's now naked cunt. Next she took the bottle of massage oil and sprinkled a little of it across the tender skin and spread it gently. She slid a pair of fingers into Sally, finding her insides as slippery as her oil covered skin. "I think you're ready for part three." Jane announced. She delved into her bag again and pulled out a giant double headed dildo.

"Where did you ever get that?" Sally asked.

"I've had it for a couple of months now. Never really had the chance to use it." The dildo bent in the middle to allow any number of positions. Jane demonstrated this by touching the two heads together. "Get undressed and maybe you can join in." Mark eagerly did as he was told.

Sally spread her legs and Jane sat between them. She lowered one end of the dildo until it tickled at Sally's naked pussy lips. "Are you ready?" she asked.

"Absolutely." Sally nodded, "But let me do this bit." She reached up and took the dildo just below its flexible middle. The whole contraption was almost two and a half feet long, and about the girth of Mark's throbbing dick. Sally placed the head to her naked lips and squeezed it in. It was slightly cold and didn't have the pulse of a real man, but it slid easily in. After a moment of sighing Sally pulled it out and fed it back again. She closed her legs to clasp the plastic head deep inside her. Jane moved quickly to straddle Sally's thighs, trapping them between her own knees and manoeuvring the other head to her own cunt.

Jane slid down the plastic pole as far as she could, then she stretched out on top of Sally, pussy to pussy and nipple to nipple. They both spread their legs and it was Sally who reached between them to pull and push the dildo. Her hand slid up and down it, lubricated by Jane's and her own juices, before she could get a grip. Jane kissed Sally, thrusting her tongue into Sally's mouth. When Sally had started trembling so much she couldn't work the dildo any more they tried a different approach. Jane waggled her butt gently up and down and back and forwards to see if they could get any movement from that. It didn't work, but they both came at the same time regardless.

With the dildo still in each other, the girls rolled over to lie side by side. Mark came over to kneel so that his dick bobbed invitingly between their mouths. A tongue sneaked out from either side and started licking at the bulbous red head. Mark leaned forward and took hold of the dildo, beginning to gently move it back and forwards. He carried on until first Jane and then Sally came, then sat up.

The girls moved to change positions again, Sally on hands and knees over Jane on her back. The dildo still connected them as Jane licked at Mark's balls while Sally kissed the end of his knob then took it into her mouth. She pooled saliva then reached around and urged him to move gently back and forth as though he were fucking her mouth. He emptied his balls into her throat and the semen dripped out of her mouth and down his shaft to be licked up by Jane.

They relaxed for a while. The girls stretched out on their backs facing away from each other. They formed a pair of interlinking Y shapes, their legs crossed comfortably at the knees, still joined by the dildo. Mark knelt down to one side of them, reached across and started moving the dildo. As it pushed into one cunt it pulled agonisingly out of the other. Now Mark had his first chance to look closely at Sally's shaved pussy lips, gorged with blood and puffed out around the plastic shaft as they were. Her clitoris had popped up and was even more visible than normal without any hair to hide behind. Mark bent over and took it between his lips and flicked his tongue over it. Sally came, and began an exquisite multiple orgasm. After a few seconds of screaming and flailing, she fainted away. Jane had her own multiple simply from watching.

When Sally came round she gently pulled herself off the dildo, squeaking as it finally popped out. Jane pulled her end of the plaything out of herself and held both ends up to her mouth to taste them. She pulled the sheet about herself and purred then seemed to doze off. Sally stood and shakily walked to the stairs. Mark joined her when she commented, "I'm going to have a shower, do you want to join me."

Something for the Weekend

All the way up the motorway, Sue had kept her thighs tightly together in case she oozed excitement and stained the car seat. Stephen hadn't noticed, engrossed as he was in driving, but he could have reached across and brushed her dress back to find she was only wearing the knee length socks underneath. They had booked a weekend in a house in the Lake District to get away from it all for a while, and Sue had very sexy plans for what they would do there. She had almost melted by the time they reached the lovely Market town of Keswick and picked up the keys.

The house was hidden away up a side road a few miles out of town. It was almost completely surrounded by trees, affording that little extra privacy. As soon as they had dropped off their suitcases in the kitchen they each did a tour of the house, far larger than they had expected, and rendezvoused again in the living room. Stephen reached to start unbuttoning Sue's dress. She stopped him and pushed him back gently, taking his hand and guiding him over to sit on the settee. He stared up appreciatively as Sue herself released the buttons of her dress. One by one they parted, her fingers shaking more the further down she got. Eventually the dress hung split but unopened. Stephen gasped and Sue knew he had just spotted her nudity beneath the dress. She smiled, thinking of his feasting on the view of her pubis, warm and lubricated and just tingling for him.

Sue turned away from Stephen, stared out of the large window as she slid the dress off her shoulder. He shifted and made appreciative noises as he studied the way her long blonde hair fell over the muscles of her back and then down to her buttocks. She moved her legs to jiggle the twin globes, then looked back over her shoulder to smile. Stephen was reaching out to stroke her lower back and bum. She stepped back, Stephen stroked down and over the twin curves and down one leg then the other to the socks.

Stephen knelt behind Sue. He kissed both buttocks then licked the sensitive triangle of flesh just above them. Sue shivered and spread her legs. Stephen's hands smoothed up the outside of Sue's legs and then around her waist. They traced their way down her stomach and teasingly around the hair of her cunt. They sneaked around again and up the inside of her thighs, this time teasing at the curls. The fingers came away damp. Stephen reached up to her waist again and twisted her to face him. He buried his face in her pubic hair and kissed the warm, damp lips.

Sue ran her fingers through Stephen's short black hair, arching her back to grind herself against his mouth. His tongue sneaked out and licked the length of her lips, flicking twice against her clitoris at the end of the journey. Sue squealed, almost falling on top of Stephen. He held her steady and supported some of her weight. "Can.... can I sit down?" she asked.

Stephen twirled her around and perched her on the side of the settee. He ran his marvellous fingers up each thigh. He ran a finger along the outside of her cunt lips, tracing the route his tongue had just taken. The finger pushed in slightly deeper and split the lips from top to bottom. They pouted red and ragged with excitement at him, twitching in time with her accelerating heart. "Put it in, please. Don't tease me." Sue squeaked.

Stephen's finger edged into Sue, she could feel every millimetre of it. Its progression was smooth, though Sue knew she was clasped tight around it. They both watched, rapt, as the finger was swallowed entirely. Stephen twisted his hand around and Sue could imagine the friction of every single ridge and whorl against her insides. He drew his finger out and then pushed it back in, angling it to put greater pressure on her clitoris. Sue threw one then the other leg over Stephen's shoulder, drawing him in closer. She whimpered when he removed his finger, only to sigh as he ducked his head between her legs again. She drew him in tighter with her legs. He nuzzled deeper between her lips, pushing the flat of his tongue against her clitoris. The orgasm that had been building mentally all day and physically for the last few minutes released and shook Sue's body. It vibrated against Stephen's tongue as he tasted her juices and shivered from her thighs to his shoulders.

Stephen slid Sue's legs from his shoulders and laid his head on her belly as aftershocks shook it. She curled around him and kissed him on the back of the neck. Her breathing steadied again and she sat back. She pushed him back to lie on the floor and straddled his legs. Her thighs still vibrated to the excitement, she wondered how ludicrous she looked, wearing only long black socks and shoes and kneeling over a fully clothed man. She reached up and unfastened Stephen's belt, then unbuttoned his trousers and rolled her hand back to feel his erection. When she unzipped the trousers, the hard on, still clothed in boxer shorts, popped out to greet her.

Sue pulled the trousers and shorts down to Stephen's ankles and inspected the treasures she had revealed. The bulbous head was turning from pink to red at the end of the rigid shaft as she ran a finger along its length. At the base an explosion of dark and curly hair hid a pair of balls in a taut scrotum. Sue stroked at the skin of the sack and it relaxed, dropping both balls into her hand.

Sue ran her fingers up the ridge along the underside of Stephen's cock, circling her fingers just above the flap of skin that connected the dome to the foreskin. Pulled taut this formed a double curve that reminded her of the top of a cartoon heart. Stephen shivered, when she glanced at him Sue could see he was watching her intently, his eyes following her every move, particularly where she came into contact with him.

Sue pushed up Stephen's T shirt and leaned forward until her lips were an inch away from his glans. She looked up his body and smiled, then reached out her tongue and teased the tip against the heart shaped top of his knob. His back arched and he hissed his breath in then released it in a low "Oooooh." Just for a moment he wasn't watching her. Sue hooked a finger under the erection and pulled it away from his stomach almost to her mouth. She licked her lips, summoned up some saliva and then licked them again.

Stephen's cock was warm, and a deeper red than the lips that slid over it. Sue fed the knob into her mouth before stopping. She licked the sensitive tip. Stephen sighed and reached out to stroke her shoulder in anticipation. Encouraged by this, Sue took some more of him into her mouth. The tip grazed along the back of her throat and she pulled back before she began to gag.

The kneading sensation of the inside of Sue's mouth had the same effect on Stephen as his tongue licking against her clitoris. He grasped at the pile of the carpet and tensed the muscles of his legs to keep from squirming and spoiling the moment by thrusting into her mouth. Sue could taste salty pre-cum in her saliva. She dipped her head as far down his shaft as she could and then lifted from it. Holding the now glistening cock in her hand, Sue began gently to rub it. Her hand slid up and down, lubricated by her own spittle. Stephen was taking deep breaths and letting them out as long, appreciative sighs.

Sue wanted to lift herself and become impaled upon the warm red rod she held, but wanted even more to see the expression on Stephen's face when he came. He threw his head back and breathed in ever shorter, sharper bursts. With a final catch in Stephen's breathing, sticky white juice exploded between Sue's fingers. It shot up his stomach, into his belly button and the hair that surrounded it. Sue rubbed a little more as more of the juice dribbled out.

Sue removed her hand, she examined the spittle and come that covered it. Stephen was relaxing into the carpet under her, but managed to reach up to offer the use of his T shirt. When Sue had cleaned her fingers to her satisfaction Stephen used the shirt himself to wipe down his belly, though this wasn't as effective. He reached up and pulled Sue's mouth to his own. They rolled over to lie side by side. Stephen pulled Sue in close and ran his hand over her back and buttocks. She relished the stickiness between them.

After a while they parted. Stephen pulled his trousers up and offered Sue a lift from the floor. To her surprise he swept her off her feet and carried her up the stairs to the bedroom.

He laid her on the edge of the bed. Sue lay back as he removed her shoes and pulled down her socks. When these were on the floor, Stephen stood and removed his sticky top. Sue looked at him and smiled. He had a good body, an even balance of regular exercise and more than enough food. His muscles were well defined, but there was also enough fat to see him through a week of cold nights. Sue had always liked that for some reason. It showed that he valued his food and related pleasures as much as his physique, neither too vain nor too much of a slob. Sue realised her mind was wandering, but a glance at the bulge in Stephen's trousers brought her back to reality. She sat up and reached out for his belt.

Stephen played with Sue's nipples as she kissed his chest and navel and fumbled blindly with the belt. The soft hairs tickled her nose and cheeks so that she almost giggled. Stephen kissed the back of her head, stroked her arms. The belt flapped open and Sue started tugging at the button and zip whilst stroking the bulge. The trousers were followed by his boxer shorts to rest around his ankles. Stephen kicked them off and threw his socks after them, then pushed Sue further back onto the bed and moved to kneel above her.

Stephen lowered himself slowly and Sue felt the length of his hard on press against her. The base rested against her clitoris and she could feel his balls gently bouncing against her labia. They smiled at each other and kissed. Sue ran a hand down Stephen's back and clasped a buttock. He shifted his weight, pushing harder at her clit. Sue made appreciative mews at the back of her throat, reaching down to play with his balls.

They enjoyed the slow dry humping for a while, before Stephen shifted himself back and lifted himself above Sue slightly. She smiled at him before reaching down to grip his cock and guide it gently into her. She could already feel the trembling in her thighs that heralded an approaching orgasm. "I want you inside me. I want you inside me now."

Stephen was eager to oblige. The glans of his hard on was as large as before. It teased against her lips and squeezed its way in. Sue could feel the ridge pressing against the walls of her cunt as it slid along them. The further in he went the further back she drew her legs, allowing him that little bit deeper. Eventually she threw her legs around his waist and drew herself up with them to pull the last of his length into her. "Oh God you're big. Oh, but I've got you all in." She caught her breath, realised that her cheeks were bright red from excitement.

Stephen drew out slowly, then pushed back in. Sue came on his second strong, slow thrust. Her vaginal and pelvic muscles vibrated with the pleasure and her thighs tautened and loosened so she throbbed against and up and down Stephen's shaft. He made a low sound of appreciation, pushing in a little harder, grinding against her clitoris and keeping her suspended in this state of delight. He drew out and pushed in again and no sooner had Sue come down from one orgasm but she felt another mounting.

Stephen pushed on, building his speed. Sue came again, and again, so often and so intensely that she lost count. She let her legs drop to the bed, spreading them as wide as they would go. Stephen lifted himself so he was only touching the bed with his hands and toes. This changed the angle of his entry, pushing the whole length of his shaft against her clitoris for the whole of each thrust. Sue was crying out with the intensity of it all, but Stephen's thrusts were speeding up as he approached his own orgasm. He pushed hard into her once more before coming, pumping into her and collapsing with a cry of his own. His cock twitched inside Sue. She could feel their juices mixing and dribbling out of her onto the blanket.

＊ ＊ ＊

Sue and Stephen had met in the bustle of a student pub on a Friday night. They had each been with their own group of friends, getting nostalgic for University daze after a week of boring work. They had exchanged a joke at the bar, then discovered they were sitting at adjoining tables. As their friends went to the toilet or bought their own rounds Sue and Stephen had moved steadily closer together. Stuck at the far ends of their respective tables, stranded from the main conversations, they made small talk. It wasn't until closing time that they discovered their friends had subtly melted away, leaving them together.

Sue had taken Stephen back to her studio flat, only a few streets away. She had turned the frame for her futon from a bed to a seat. They had kicked off their shoes and talked and drank decaffeinated coffee until she fell asleep just as Saturday was dawning. When she woke at noon she was curled up with her head in Stephen's lap. He was stroking her hair, back then it had only reached down to her shoulders. She would have liked to sit up sharply and look offended, but the feeling of his fingers parting the strands was just too sensual.

Sue lifted herself slowly from Stephen's lap. "I can't believe I went to sleep with you still here. You could have done anything."

Stephen smiled at her, "I was brought up to always ask permission first." Sue massaged the crick in her neck. Stephen reached across, gently moved her hand aside and soothed the muscle with expert fingers. At that moment he could have asked permission to do anything to Sue and she would have said yes. She stood up quickly and walked into the kitchen, turning the kettle on and checking the fridge for milk.

"Would you like some breakfast?" Sue asked Stephen, shouting so he could hear her in the living room.

"Just a coffee, please." he said from right behind her. She squealed in shock and spurted milk all over her face and blouse from the open carton. When she turned to face him there was a drop of white liquid dangling from the end of her nose. Stephen was gentleman enough to fight back his amusement. He spotted a roll of kitchen towel and tore off a piece to wipe her face dry. "Your blouse is soaked, you should probably take it off." He suggested.

"Oh really, and would you like to watch?"

"With your permission." Stephen allowed himself a little smile as he threw the wet towel into the bin. On an impulse Sue kissed him. It had only been meant as a light peck, but became a melting battle of tongues and lips. Stephen's arms on her hips kept Sue's wet blouse at a safe distance but the rest of his body strived to touch her.

Sue broke off the kiss and stepped back. "You have my permission to watch me undress." She reached up and released the top button of her blouse. The others parted slowly and she found herself gyrating to a rhythm she was making up. Eventually she slid her arms out of the wet blouse and dumped it on the floor.

Sue was happy to remember that she had put on her sexiest black bra, even though that meant it too was wet. She stepped closer to Stephen and turned slowly, offering the catch to him. He released it then slid the straps off her shoulders and let it fall to the floor. Sue crossed her arms over her breasts and turned, smiling. "Okay," she announced, "you can only watch me take off the rest of my clothes if you take off all of yours." Stephen considered this for a moment, then quickly unbuttoned his shirt and tossed it out into the hall. He unbuckled his belt and unzipped his trousers. Sue didn't object when he let the trousers drop to his ankles, so he pulled them and his socks off and tossed them after his shirt. Sue gestured at his boxer shorts, keeping her other arm across her breasts, "Go on then, everything." The erection within the shorts pushed outwards insistently.

Stephen took Sue's hand and pulled her closer. He placed her hand on his waist, just above the elasticated band of the boxers. "I thought you might want to do that."

It was a job she could clumsily complete with one hand, but it deserved her full attention. Sue placed her other hand on Stephen's waist, revealing her breasts to him for the first time. He looked down and smiled at the erect nipples, she pushed both hands inside the waistband of his boxers and stroked the hair on his thighs. They kissed again, and as their tongues played, Stephen's hands came up to cup Sue's breasts and hers reached around to clasp his erection. She pushed the boxer shorts down his thighs and let them fall to his feet, he found the buttons on the back of her skirt and began releasing them. The skirt dropped to Sue's feet and revealed her black panties and the elasticated top of her stockings.

Stephen stepped out of his boxers and led Sue into the living room. He sat her down on the futon and knelt before her, then began placing kisses up and down her arms and neck. Sue sank back in the seat and closed her eyes, savouring the luxurious attention. Stephen kissed her collar bone, then moved down to the rise of her breasts. Her nipples were jutting out, just waiting for him, hot and tender. But he skipped over them and moved down to lick around her navel.

Sue giggled at the novelty of Stephen's tongue moving around and into her belly button, treating it like a miniature vagina. He moved up again, kissing up to her ribs and then the bottom of her breasts. Now he found her nipples, cooling them down and making them yet harder with his mouth. He drew one up to a sharper, tighter point, then moved on to the other. Sue could feel little shivers of orgasm building in her body. She clasped Stephen tight to her breast and wrapped her legs around his back. She climaxed, letting out a musical screaming sigh. Shudders of joy ran through her body, along her arms and legs and gently back, slowly subsiding.

Stephen kissed Sue's belly and gently stroked her arms as he let her sink back onto the futon. He sat back on his haunches with a satisfied expression, pleased that he could create such ecstasy in another person. His erection was taut against his belly, demanding attention. Sue wanted to jump on it and ride it until he screamed just as she had. And she would, just as soon as she had the energy. She slid a hand down her belly and into the waistband of her panties. Her cunt was slippery slick with her arousal, she slipped a finger into it.

Sue stood slowly and pushed her panties down her legs. Stephen leaned closer and sniffed her honey blonde pubic hair. Then he reached out his tongue and licked the length of her glistening lips. She sighed and placed both hands on his head, holding him close as a finger traced up the inside of her thigh and slowly into the depths of her vagina. She wanted to slide down his body onto his dick and stay joined to him there for the rest of the day. But there was something missing.

"Do you have condoms?" Sue asked, as casually as she could manage. A second finger had sneaked into her and she was trying hard not to press down on the pair of them.

Stephen sat back and removed his fingers. Sue cursed. "No. Sorry."

"Damn." She had thrown away an out of date packet just the week before, lamenting her lack of opportunities to have used them. "I'll have to get some." At first Sue was surprised that this brought a smile to Stephen's face, then realised she had just made it clear what they would be doing for the rest of the day.

Sue bent down to draw her panties back up, but Stephen caught them and held them on the floor. "Now you don't really need those, do you." He grinned. It was an infectious grin and it dared her to go outside naked under whatever clothes she did put on.

"No, I guess I don't." Sue grinned back. She stepped out of the panties and went into the hall. She picked up her skirt and Stephen's shirt. The shirt was a little too large, she rolled up the sleeves to her elbows. She fastened the skirt and moved it until the slit wouldn't make her nakedness too obvious, then she grabbed her purse and hurried out of the flat.

There was a small shop on the corner of the building which stayed open twenty four hours and stocked everything a person could need. But the staff all knew Sue and she didn't want them smiling at her purchase, no matter that some of them would simply be happy for her. Further up the street was a chemists she hardly ever went into. As she headed towards it a light breeze found its way into her skirt and whispered through her wet pubes. It was so cool against her blood warmed lips that she shivered with joy. She became hotter still and could feel the juices slicking the inside of her thighs.

Sue stopped short of the chemist's and thought of rearranging the shirt she wore. She knew her face was red from excited embarrassment and must look dishevelled and ravished. The staff would know what she had been doing, the thought thrilled her. She pushed open the door and stepped into the chemist's.

The condoms were on the counter, Sue bought the largest pack she could find and left quickly. She clutched her purse and the paper chemist's bag tight and walked back to her block briskly. Once inside she ran up the stairs and was practically breathless by the time she reached her own flat.

Sue locked the door behind herself and rushed into the main room. Stephen had folded the futon out into a bed and was lying on it. He leapt up and grabbed Sue as she came through the door. They kissed and fell back onto the bed. Stephen slid a hand up the inside of his borrowed shirt to cup Sue's breasts, then reached down and slid the skirt up her thigh to expose her bush, glistening with her juices.

Sue pushed the purse away and ripped open the chemist's bag. She tore the cellophane off the box and pulled out a condom. Stephen had a finger inside her and she was finding it hard to concentrate. The foil wrapper came off and the sheath rolled down Stephen's hard cock. He cupped one of her buttocks in each hand and rolled her onto her back, moving above her. He didn't need guiding, she was soaking, open wide and inviting. They both gasped as Stephen slid smoothly in to the hilt. Sue climaxed immediately, and clung to Stephen with arms and legs.

They took a moment to enjoy the feeling of being so close, filled and filling. Then Sue reached down and pulled her skirt up around her waist. They kissed and she relaxed into the bed, one hand idly unbuttoning the shirt. Stephen's mouth explored the crook of her neck, her ears and her hairline. His hand stroked along her thigh, guiding it to hook over his waist. Without being told, she knew what he intended. They rolled onto their sides still as close together as was possible.

They had made love like this for an hour, hardly moving, giving attention to parts of each other's bodies other lovers would have ignored in the rush. Eventually, Sue had rolled Stephen onto his back. She had thrown off the shirt and ridden up and down his cock, her skirt a tent hiding their sexes from view. They didn't leave the house for the rest of the weekend. The following week they had gone to the doctor, had a few precautionary tests, and Sue had gone on the Pill. That had been two years ago. They had moved into a larger flat together a year ago and were getting married at the end of the summer. To celebrate, they had vowed to explore all the possibilities of sex that they could, starting this weekend.

* * *

They woke early the next day, still in the habit of rising for work. The rental on the house had included a canoe and a pair of bikes. Stephen wanted to take the canoe and explore Derwent water, landing on islands he had found on a map. After a light breakfast they strapped the canoe to the roof rack and set out.

They drove first to Keswick. Whilst Stephen shopped for picnic food, Sue went to a few other shops for supplies of her own. The sun hid briefly behind the clouds and she worried that perhaps she was going to be under dressed in shorts and a light blouse almost sheer enough to show her nipples. By the time she got back to the car it was sunny again. Stephen was waiting in the driver's seat, putting food into a bag with the picnic gear. Sue carefully put her bag of supplies behind her seat.

They drove to a launch site on the shore of Derwent Water. Stephen carried the canoe and food bag to the shore whilst Sue struggled with the paddles and buoyancy aids as well as her own bag. She kicked her shoes off and put them in the canoe as they pushed off. "Where are we going?" she asked as they got into the swing of paddling.

"Over there." Stephen pointed out an island and began steering towards it.

"Is it inhabited?"

"If we're lucky, no." Stephen had a wicked grin.

They set up a steady stroke, crossing the slightly choppy lake, but Sue shivered as the wind cut through her top. She rested her paddle behind her seat and laid a buoyancy aid in front of it, then stretched out on it below the gunnels and out of the wind. The sun shone directly onto her and she was warm again quickly. She couldn't quite reach Stephen's crotch with her bare foot, but she waved it enticingly in front of him until he leant forward and nibbled a toe.

"How far to the island now." Sue asked after five minutes.

"Not far at all."

"And is there anybody on it?"

"Nope."

"Goody. I need to top up my tan." Sue trailed her hand in the water. It was cold, so she decided to put aside her original plan of swimming to the island. She checked the distance to the island and began unbuttoning her blouse. This went in the bag with the towels and food. Stephen pulled the paddle up and reached it across to dribble water onto Sue's navel. She squealed and squirmed and giggled and dipped her hand into the water to splash back.

Stephen dipped the paddle back into the lake and splashed water against the side of the boat. "Ah, ah, now. Let's not have escalation, I can shift much more water than you."

"Damn. Oh okay." Sue subsided and hooked her thumbs under the waistband of her shorts. She lifted her buttocks and slid the shorts down her legs. The slip of material followed the blouse into the bag. Sue hooked her knees over the gunnels and trailed her feet in the water. As the sun played upon the blonde hair around her crack she felt a different warmth spreading from inside it.

The rocking of the boat was sensual and the steady paddle relaxing. Sue closed her eyes and sighed. She felt her cunt lips pouting open as she imagined Stephen staring at her, or the surprise of anybody upon another boat seeing her naked in the canoe. The paddling stopped briefly and Stephen lightly brushed the inside of Sue's thigh then ran fingers through her pubic hair. "Brace yourself." he told her. Sue opened her eyes and looked at him, confused, just as the canoe grounded on the beach and crunched against the fine pebbles.

Stephen leapt out and splashed along the side of the boat. He dragged it a short way up the beach then leant in to kiss Sue. She reached up and stroked the back of his neck as he cupped a breast. They parted and Stephen picked up the bag. Sue stepped out of the canoe and pulled it a little further up the beach.

They found a clearing just at the top of the beach which caught the sun but was shielded from the wind and view. Stephen laid out a rug and the towel and started emptying the food onto it. Sue curled her legs under herself and leant against a tree, reaching into her bag to get some suntan lotion. She started spreading the lotion on her arms as Stephen began laying out cooked ham on paper plates. When she smoothed the lotion over her breasts the nipples stood erect and sensitive.

Stephen broke lumps of French bread and put it onto the plates. He shuffled closer to Sue and handed her a plate. "Why don't you get undressed as well, I'm sure an all over tan would suit you." Stephen smiled agreement and slid out of his light trousers, boxers and T-shirt. He placed his plate on his lap, out of necessity rather than coyness. Sue spread lotion over her stomach and legs and began to eat.

When they had cleared the first phase of food, Sue began to root around in the bag. Stephen took the suntan lotion and squirted a little on her back and began gently massaging it over her shoulders and down to her buttocks. When he ran out he squirted yet more into the triangular cleft above Sue's buttocks. She shivered with unexpected pleasure, and again as a cold trickle ran between the cleft of her buttocks and pooled briefly at her anus. She lowered her head to the ground as Stephen smoothed the lotion over her buttocks and the backs of her thighs. Her cunt lips were pouting at him again and he teased them with his little finger.

Sue pushed the food bag aside and lowered herself to lie on the rug. Stephen was rubbing around her upper thighs and buttocks again, teasingly brushing the skin between her vagina and anus. She purred and thrust her buttocks back into the air slightly. "Darling, there's..... can you do something for me?"

"Of course." Stephen dipped a finger into her vagina, bringing it back out again before she could nip at it.

"In my bag there's some lubricant. I'd like you to.... I want to experience something new..... Would you....." Stephen paused in his stroking briefly. There was a rustle as he pulled the bag over and reached inside. Sue was certain he knew what she meant, but felt that she had to say it so he was sure. Before she said anything there was a finger rubbing up between her buttocks, spreading them and teasing at her anus. "That's it, yes. I want to try anal sex." It sounded more exciting than disgusting when she said it now.

Stephen moved around behind Sue. She could feel his erection slip and fit between her buttocks. It moved away again and cold liquid spurted from a tube into her buttock cleft. She shivered with delight when she realised it wasn't the suntan lotion. Stephen's finger played with the lubricant, marshalling it to her anus, rubbing around it and then gently pushing into the entrance. The finger pushed in to the first joint then pulled out. Sue shivered with delight as Stephen squirted more gel between her buttocks and some flowed into the dilated hole. Stephen fingered the cold liquid to Sue's ring-piece and pushed in again, this time to the second joint. She gasped with delight at the confusing sensations as the finger probed around the inside of her back passage.

Stephen had moved such that the head of his erection teased at Sue's cunt lips. It slid in with ease, surprising her with how damp she was. Stephen withdrew his finger and pushed his dick deeper into Sue in the same movement. More liquid squirted into Sue's crack, more flowed into her hole. This time she was surprised to find two fingers making their way into her. At first she wanted to tense against this larger invasion, but relaxed under Stephen's gentle insistence. Both fingers slid into her, slowly, as far as they could go. Sue found she was panting. Stephen pulled his dick from her and she whimpered. He twisted his fingers and pushed them further into her and she whimpered again, a little noise of new pleasure.

Stephen withdrew his fingers and spurted some more of the gel around Sue's anus. She tried to remain relaxed and shivered with pleasure as the liquid flowed down her open bum hole. For a few moments she lay there, feeling more open and more deliciously vulnerable than she ever had before. Then Stephen clasped her buttock cheeks and prised them wider open, pulling the hole to another limit, and something poked around the entrance to her arse. It was too thick to be a finger, and anyway, both hands were elsewhere. It was some time before Sue's pleasure dazed mind could understand what was invading her. The head of Stephen's dick had forced past Sue's sphincter before she clenched the muscle in surprise. She bit her lip, fearing she had hurt Stephen, but got a low murmur of, "Wow" instead.

Sue tried to relax, and Stephen was sliding in on the heavy lubrication he had squirted over his dick and pushed into the tight passage. He brought a hand round to tease at Sue's clitoris and vagina, she only managed to vaguely hope it wasn't the same hand as had just been probing her arse. The hand withdrew as Stephen began pumping away, he had to hold her waist so as to stop her rocking too violently under his thrusts.

Sue spotted a carrot in amongst the food that was left. She groped for it through a daze and brought it back to push into her vagina. The vegetable slid slowly into her, its wrinkled texture teasing at her clitoris. Sue came, there was a burst of bright light behind her eyes. She released the carrot and found that it moved inside her in time to Stephen's thrusts, keeping her perpetually at the peak of orgasm. She found herself crying out, the sound seemed to come from far away. It was joined by sounds of exertion and joy from Stephen as he approached orgasm. Fleetingly, Sue remembered how well sound carried over water and imagined people on the shore being able to hear these wild sounds without knowing where they came from.

With a cry, Stephen came. Liquid spurted further up into Sue than she had imagined possible and she revelled in the feel of it running through her. She shivered all over with her ongoing orgasm, collapsing to the ground with Stephen on top of her, careful only that the carrot didn't push any further into her. Stephen breathed heavily in her ear. He began to pull out slowly, slipping easily with all the lubrication. There was a roll of tissue in Sue's bag, Stephen used it to wipe up the liquid that dribbled from her and then to clean his tender cock. All the while Sue lay before him shivering with after pleasure and the glorious sensation of the vegetable still in her. Stephen kissed each cheek of her buttocks, then the triangle just above them before lifting her to slowly pull out the carrot.

Rolling Sue gently onto her side, Stephen spotted tears drying on her cheeks. He moved up and closer to her, "I'm sorry. I didn't hurt you did I?"

Sue blushed, and tried to hide it by pulling the carrot slowly and enticingly to her lips. She teased the end of the vegetable with her tongue, tasting herself on it, then took a couple of inches into her mouth. When she slid all but the top half inch of the carrot out of her mouth, Sue glanced up at Stephen. He was watching, rapt, with a sly grin on his face. Sue smiled around the orange root, then bit the end off. Stephen flinched, an exaggerated look of pain crossing his face. "Let's go for a swim." Sue suggested.

They couldn't really swim. The lake shelved away steeply quite close to the shore and the water was very cold, so they sat in the water to their waists and washed themselves. When they walked back to the rug, Sue laughed at how small Stephen had become from the cold. She gave herself a brisk rub down with the towel and then made Stephen lie back on the rug to dry him off.

Sue rubbed the towel down one of Stephen's legs and then the other, then she leaned over him and breathed on his shrunken penis. He smiled as he warmed up, Sue kissed around his cock and balls as they came back into the open. Sue licked along the ridge on the underside of the growing hard on. It stretched under her attention until it stood up from Stephen's stomach and the foreskin pulled off the purple head. Sue licked at the sensitive dimple where the foreskin met the head, then took the end into her mouth.

Lying at Stephen's side was the food bag. Poking enticingly out of the bag was another carrot. Sue reached across and pulled it out, never letting Stephen out of her mouth and even transferring the move into a slurp along his shaft, and examined it. The vegetable was a couple of inches shorter than Stephen's dick and not as thick. Releasing Stephen's hard on and sitting up, Sue waved the carrot at him and picked up the half full tube of lubricant to make her point. Stephen bit his lower lip and looked a little worried, then relaxed and smiled, "Why not. New experiences, eh?"

They shuffled around until Stephen was kneeling. Sue lay in front of him and rested her shoulders on his thighs, she could lift her head to take his cock in her mouth and reach around behind him to play with his arsehole. Licking at the base of the shaft to distract him, Sue squirted lubricant onto her finger and then played it into Stephen's anus. She repeated this three times before squirting gel over the carrot and bringing it to bear. As the cold vegetable teased at his ring-piece, Stephen tensed. Sue lifted her head and took his knob into her mouth. Stephen sighed, then gasped as the carrot slid into him.

Sue set up a rhythm. As she pushed the carrot in, she would swallow as much of Stephen as possible. Then when she pulled it out until only the end was in, she would slurp back to hold only the end of the cock in her lips. Stephen continually groaned with pleasure and could barely contain the thrusts he wanted to make down Sue's throat. Before long she could tell that his orgasm was mounting and released the carrot to clasp his buttocks as she swallowed more of him than she would have thought possible. Carried away by deep throating, Sue went beyond the gag reflex and set up her breathing almost unconsciously. Stephen gasped as the carrot slid most of the way out, resting on the ground and still probing him with every move and shiver. He cried out as he came, Sue swallowed all of the salty liquid that dribbled rather than spurted against the back of her throat.

They collapsed onto their sides on the rug. Sue let the softening dick out of her mouth and moved up to kiss Stephen. They cuddled together and savoured the warmth of the sun on their bodies. "I love you." Stephen told Sue, kissing her on the forehead.

Life Drawing

"Take all your clothes off and lie on the bed." Mark did as he was told, lying on his back with hands clasped behind his head watching Sally as she bustled about the room. She picked up a sketch pad, some pencils and charcoal and an eraser, then brought a seat around to the side of the bed and positioned herself so she had a good view of Mark's crotch. "I never did get around to doing this." She announced, "Now I am going to sketch your darling dick."

Mark closed his eyes and listened to the sound of a pencil on paper and the steady breathing Sally used when she was concentrating. After five minutes the chair creaked as she sat back in it. "Not at all bad, even if I do say so myself." She commented. Mark opened his eyes and smiled approvingly at the picture she held up to him. His resting penis, snug in its foreskin, nestled in the curls of his pubic hair. Sally turned the page over and put the pad and pencils aside for a moment. "That's Doctor Jekyll, now it's time to do Mister Hyde." She said, hooking a slim finger under Mark's dick. It began to rise at her attentions, then grew even more quickly when she flicked her tongue over the tip. She took the end in her mouth and swallowed as much of it as she could as it neared its full length.

Sally picked up the pad and pencils again and sat down when she was satisfied that Mark was up to his full fighting length. "There now, do you think you can keep it up until I've finished my sketch?" she asked.

"Maybe. But I could do even better with a little encouragement." Mark smiled as he said this. Sally joined in the joke, standing and releasing her short dress. She flashed her shaved pussy at Mark, then dipped a finger between her legs and was surprised by how wet it was when it came back. She took the finger and presented it to Mark, who licked it and sucked it into his mouth. "That should do it." He said.

Sally sketched Mark's erection quickly. Watching her he could see that her concentration was now mixed with more than a little excitement. After two minutes she stopped and, for no readily apparent reason, leaned forward and kissed the tip of his dick then went back to her sketching. When she had finished she presented the picture to Mark. For a moment he had a vision of his erection as a very frightening Loch Ness monster. When he looked again it took shape on the page and he smiled. "That's me?" Sally nodded and turned the page over again. She put the pad aside and took off her top and bra, presenting first one and then the other nipple to Mark to lick. She came quickly and kissed him all over his face and neck.

"There's only one natural progression for this set of sketches." Sally announced. She went to the mirror on the wall and brought it back. She couldn't find any way to prop it up on the end of the bed, so she had Mark turn around so that his feet pointed to the wall. The mirror sat against the wall and reflected Mark's dick just the way Sally wanted it to. She kissed him and picked up her pad and pencils again. Carefully she straddled Mark's thighs facing towards his feet and the mirror. For the first time she had the view of her shaved pussy that others had and it excited her. She reached her free hand down and split the lips, looking at the glistening insides. She moved back and slid the wet lips along Mark's dick, then lifted it and slid down it.

"Don't move now, you'll spoil my sketching." Sally told Mark, who groaned at the self control. Sally tried to concentrate on the image in the mirror and ignore the dick deep inside her. It was hard, and when Mark seemed to be shifting slightly under her she stopped sketching and used her muscle exercises to keep him still and give him a little pleasure in payment. The longer she kept still the more insistent the pulse of Mark's dick became and the more she wanted to move. Sally had started sketching the most important part of the picture, where penis and vagina met, and this was the most detailed. The rest of the picture became scratchy and indistinct by comparison. She could feel her orgasm building from the sensual movement of pencil on paper and came before she had even finished the drawing. Eventually she was satisfied with what she had drawn and she threw aside the pad and began riding Mark. He grasped her waist and held her steady as he added his own thrusts from underneath. Sally pictured his movements in her as an animation, a pencilled dick on grainy paper and her naked pussy highlighted with just a little bit of red. She came again as Mark pumped semen into her.

Sally sank down beside Mark. She found the pad and showed the last sketch to him. He began to rise just looking at it. "The things an artist must do to achieve her vision." He commented. Sally kissed and nuzzled his neck and reached down to stroke his sticky half hard dick.

"Maybe my model will have to make a few sacrifices," Sally whispered in Mark's ear, "because I want to draw a lot of different positions. You might have to pose with Jane."

"Oh dear, the hardship. That is, of course, if David will let me."

"He's not possessive is he?"

"I don't think so, but I reckon he'll be as eager to model as me."

Mark was hard again now. Sally looked at her hand then licked it. "You're all sticky, let me just clean you up." She suggested, and her tongue was licking along the sides of Mark's prick in a second. She lapped the sticky mix of semen and other juices like a cat and left him glistening with her saliva and even harder than before. "Now, whatever shall I do with this? I know, you just put it here between my tits and see what happens." Sally rolled onto her back and guided Mark's dick around until it rested in her cleavage. She squeezed her breasts together so that they closed over it and Mark began moving it backwards and forwards. Wet as it was from her licking it slid easily between the mammaries which held it.

At the top of each thrust Mark's dick came close to Sally's mouth. She reached out her tongue and teased the tip each time. The movement of her breasts stimulated her nipples up to peaks and she could feel an orgasm rising as Mark's movements became faster and more ragged. When he came Mark spurted semen into her mouth, over her chin and neck and between her breasts. Sally hadn't quite reached orgasm, but she came quickly when he began lapping the sticky juices from her tits and throat.

First Contact

I have to admit, the music isn't really to my taste. Simply Red is a bit dull, but they consider it the stuff to make love to. I don't complain, I'm the guest and they are the hosts. He is in the shower, she is naked on the bed, one hand playing with small breasts, the other sliding through the lubricated folds of her cunt. I am sitting in the wicker chair at the foot of the bed, still fully clothed but for my shoes. We are watching the large screen video of her husband pumping hard and regular into her arse.

The sound of the shower stops and he comes into the bedroom wearing a white towelling bathrobe and rubbing his wet hair. He is half bald, so it doesn't take very long. "Hell," he says, "you're still dressed. You don't have to stand on ceremony son, she hasn't." We both look at his wife, maybe half his age and hot as hell, as she sits up to look at us. She smiles, she is about to get a show and then I am going to fuck her. I am going to fuck her, but first I have to satisfy her husband. I stand and take off my shirt and release my hard on from my trousers. He smiles and strokes my arse as I bend over to take the trousers off. This is it, soon I will be bi-curious no longer.

I turn back to him and he slides the robe from his shoulders. He is an inch or so shorter than me and slightly tubby, his belly isn't so large that it overwhelms his dick where it throbs and pulses out of his crotch. I kneel before him and for the first time see another man's cock right up close. I lick along the underside then tease the sensitive tip of the glans, just like I would want it. Then I lick my lips and pool saliva in my mouth. With one hand around the shaft, so he can't thrust too far in, I take a breath and gulp on the head.

The knob tastes of soap and man. I never believed it would be this exciting, I move my hands and bob my head up and down, pushing it into me as far as I can. He starts fucking my mouth, slowly and gently, hands on my shoulders. She is moaning as she watches, I can't see her, but I know she is being driven wild by this. He pulls out of my mouth, saliva dripping down his shaft. "Fuck her," he commands, "and I'll fuck you."

She lies back on the edge of the bed, feet flat on the floor, and splits her labia, inviting me in. Her husband and I put on our condoms and he begins to lube his up. I slide into her as far as I can and take a nipple into my mouth.

She reaches down and clasps my butt cheeks, pulling them apart. I can feel him behind me and try to relax before his assault.

The tip of his cock pushes at the edge of my sphincter and I clench it unconsciously. It is cold, then it is warm, then it is hard, insistent. I relax and he pushes, lodging the head and making me gasp. She wraps her legs around mine, holding me as her husband pushes slowly in. I can feel myself in her, feel him in me, taste him on my tongue. I faint away.

When I wake I'm hearing gasps and moans, and I realise they include mine and no longer just the video. He isn't large, a few more moments and I could have swallowed him whole, but I can feel him pushing against my insides. The butt plug was never like this.

She kisses me across the forehead and licks my eyebrows and shows me that she has been training her cunt. "Don't move, let the old man do all the work." she suggests. Goaded by this he pulls out very slowly, lubes up again and pushes back in even more smoothly. It moves me against her clit and she purrs. He picks up the pace and it is beginning to feel beautiful.

There is a pause in the soundtrack of the video. We all look at the screen and suddenly we are watching this very same scene being played out, but with a pretty young Asian boy in my place. The boy licks her distended nipples and so do I.

He is ramming hard and fast into me now and she is screaming out with approaching orgasm. I can only pant and hang on, if I weren't so excited his hands digging into my waist would hurt. He is on his last desperate lunges and she is shivering through her second coming beneath me. He barks and I can feel him filling the sheath inside me. He pulls out and sits back on the floor.

Her legs move from their vice grip on mine and wrap around my waist. "Fuck her hard boy, make her come again." he tells me, tossing aside the full condom and stretching out on the floor where he can watch me filling her. I hook my arms under her knees and push her legs back until they touch her tits and I'm pumping as hard as I can.

She comes again, and again on and on until I've lost count. Then so am I and it is so intense that I'm fainting away again.

I can feel them gently lifting me aside and laying me out on the floor. I keep my eyes closed until I feel the condom being gently rolled off and a tongue lightly licking me clean. She is on her hands and knees lapping at me as he takes her from behind. Over his shoulder he is giving a blow job to the young Asian. I'm tender and my arse throbs beautifully and I'm getting hard again. "It's going to be a long night." he says.

Working Away

The company paid an allowance for staying away from home, but it was so low that it could never cover a decent hotel room. So I'd done some asking around, and got lucky.

Jess and Tony were friends of a friend. They had a flat in the city centre with a sofa that folded out to become a bed, and they'd be happy to let me stay for a week for half my allowance. We all got to profit from the arrangement and I was only a few minutes walk away from the office.

It was one of those expensive loft apartments. The sofa bed was in the living room, which was on the same open plan as the kitchen. Jess and Tony's bedroom was off to one side, with the bathroom beside it. They had to walk through the living room to the bathroom, but my presence didn't seem to bother them. In the morning, Jess would get up first. She was about five foot two and gorgeous. Nothing on her was more than a handful, with firm little breasts and lovely round buttocks. She would go to the bathroom in a short T-shirt and knickers. Tony would go when she got back, or join her if he felt like it. He was six foot and a bit and obviously used the gym in the building's basement. They didn't seem to know, or care, that I was always awake to watch their morning parades.

Everything went well at the office and I was going to finish on Friday, as planned. On Thursday night I cooked a meal and told Jess and Tony I'd be leaving the following evening. "Oh no, don't do that, stay a little longer." Said Jess.

"Yeah," added Tony, "Friday's a hell of a night around here. Stay over and let us show you a good time."

"Well, er, sure, why not." I didn't have anything special planned for when I got home.

When I woke up the next morning I thought the banging was in my head. It took a moment to realise the sound was from the bedroom. Jess was trying to be quiet, but couldn't keep from crying out as Tony fucked her. "Oh God, yes! Yes! Yes!" The last cry was echoed by Tony.

I stared at the door, trying to imagine those two fine bodies hard at it. The handle turned and the door swung open. Jess was standing there, stark naked.

I didn't get to find out if she was naturally blonde, because her pubes had been shaved. She gently rubbed her wet pussy lips then stretched. Tony came up behind her. He was naked too, his long, thin, half erect penis pointing at the floor a few feet ahead of him. He handed her a T-shirt and she pulled it on. They kissed and she went to the bathroom. The bedroom door closed.

* * *

I didn't know if they had seen my wide eyes. I had a hard on all day and found it tricky concentrating on my work. Luckily there wasn't much left to do and I still managed to finish early. I walked back to the flat in a daze.

Neither Jess nor Tony were in, but I had a spare key. I decided to have a shower. If they were going to take me out, I should look and smell my best. I was washing the shampoo from my hair when I heard the flat door open and movement in the living room. The bathroom door opened, I'd forgotten to lock it. "Hey there." Said Tony as he came in and started washing his hands.

"Hey." I was getting a hard on remembering what I had seen earlier. I turned away, I didn't want him getting the wrong idea.

"How's big gay Bob?" he asked of our mutual acquaintance.

"Still big. And still gay."

"He told us you were bi."

"Yeah, well, I don't, y'know. Do guys, often." I was completely hard. There was no way I could hide this.

Tony handed me a towel. "I'm just saying, because that good time we promised you? It can be on the town. Or in the bedroom. You saw us this morning?"

"Yeah."

"What did you think?"

"Gorgeous. Both of you." I turned round now. He looked down and smiled. My dick was shorter than his, but thicker. He reached out and touched it. I realised he was nervous. "Jess has always wanted to see me with another man, and I've always wanted to try it. But we've never found the right man."

He helped me out of the bath. I was a couple of inches shorter than him. I watched his face, trying to read what was needed next. He was gently tugging at my dick. Then he sank to his knees and kissed it, licked it from stem to tip then ran his tongue around the head.

Tony stood again, he turned to the cabinet, collected some tubes and bottles and walked to the door. "We'll be in the bedroom." he announced.

I dried quickly, brushed my hair and checked myself in the mirror. Wrapping a towel around my waist, I went out into the living room. The bedroom door was open and there were soft sounds of conversation coming from within.

They were both lying on the bed, naked. Jess was coaxing Tony's cock to hardness. He had his eyes closed, concentrating on the sensations. She smiled at me and gestured. I let the towel drop and walked to the bed. She eyed up my erection, then leant forward to kiss it.

We shifted round until I could take Tony's cock in my mouth and Jess could watch whilst she sucked on mine. I took as much as I could into my mouth, swirling my tongue around the head. Tony shifted and moaned. His movement presented his arsehole to me. The tubes he had taken from the bathroom were lubes. I coated a finger and slowly pushed it up his arse. I massaged his prostate and Tony squirmed with joy.

I coaxed Tony into rolling over. By now I had two fingers up his arse and he was doing whatever I asked. I signalled for Jess to take my place in front of Tony whilst I moved behind him. She went one better, presenting her pussy to him. "Be brave, lover." She whispered to him, pulling him over on top of her.

Buried to the hilt in Jess, and with her pulling his cheeks apart, Tony's arse presented a glorious target. I applied the lube liberally and pushed in. There was resistance as I eased past the sphincter, then the passage closed tight around me.

"Oh God!" Tony cried out as he came. I knew what he meant, his arse pumped my cock in time to the spurts he was pouring into Jess. I massaged his balls and started moving.

My movements rocked Tony against Jess' clit and soon she was making the same sounds of joy I had heard that morning. "Yes! Yes! Yes!!!!" She came. Moments later I was pumping semen into Tony.

We collapsed onto the bed, arranging ourselves so that Jess was between Tony and me. We stroked her little body, I pushed a finger into her pussy and massaged it. "One fantasy fulfilled." I said.

"But there are others. I want to see Tony fuck you. And I want two men at once."

"And I want to see you take Jess. And I want to give you a blow job."

"Okay, okay. Do you mind if I stay until Sunday in that case?"

Anything goes on Mars station

Amongst the problems with sex in free-fall is finding something to push against. People have thought up some incredible positions, and developed the stirrups for zero gravity play rooms such as the one we call the Heart. They're high impact plastic tubing with straps for footholds fastened to them. I pushed off the wall gently and took a stirrup to the centre of the Heart, where the bots waited. My little blue ovoid personal assistant flipped a piece of its carapace up to hook through a hole in the stirrup.

The others drifted over, bringing more stirrups and toys with them. Marc was the last to kick off from the wall. He had to put the panel back over the entry hatch and stick the "butt plug" in the vacuum hole. The Heart is cleaned with an airlock system, sucking all the fluids and other stuff through a small pipe. There are safety features galore, but the plug is one last way to be sure. I watched my buddy for the next month as he sailed over. He was short but heavily muscled. We were all more toned than when we'd set off for Mars. Electro stimulators had been exercising our muscles all the way out, whilst we hyper-slept and had our training pumped straight into our brains.. He spread his arms and legs to give us a full frontal view. His penis, already half erect, is shorter than mine, and not as thick, but attractively formed just like he is.

The others reached the group of bots and I enjoyed the feeling of all that naked flesh sliding past me. There were six of us in the shift team- me, Marc, Yuki, Shanna, Kyle and Olaf- in three buddy pairs. Each buddy team was together for thirty days at a time. There were two other shift teams, and we would swap between them as well. By the end of my tour on the Mars station I'd have buddied with all seventeen others- nine men, nine women. The buddy system had evolved over the years, from simply a way to stay safe in space to a means to bring a crew together in ways more innocent bonding methods simply couldn't. They'd had to recruit for more open minded astronauts, but that had actually increased applications. Nowadays crews didn't meet until they were in orbit over Earth, about to board the seventeen month flight to Mars. And they slept for the whole of that. We had arrived less than twelve hours ago, eager and horny, and the station's computers had made the first buddy selections. For the next shift period I would work, eat, sleep and play with Marc. Occasionally one or more of the shift crew would join us, as they all were for this first session to celebrate our arrival over Mars.

We clipped toys to our bots and they sailed away on puffs of compressed gas, ready to be called later. I grabbed the nearest handhold on Olaf, his huge erection. He grinned at me, caught Yuki's ankle and started climbing up her leg. I felt a collision with my midriff, hands wrapped around my waist and a tongue swirled around the tip of my penis. Marc had got straight to the point. I pulled myself closer to Olaf's dick and ran a tongue along the underside. Yuki had hooked her legs under his armpits and clamped her pussy to his face. All of five foot two, she was juggling six foot plus Kyle like a balloon, flicking her tongue over his hard on every time he drifted past. At the other end of our chain Yanna was kissing up the inside of Marc's thighs.

Yuki stopped teasing Kyle, grabbed his buttocks and pulled him toward her. Now we began the shifts and realignments that allowed us to form a ring, docking Shanna and Kyle. I took Olaf's dick into my mouth, savouring the flavour. Holding the base with one hand I moved around it. Marc hooked my legs over his shoulders and started rimming me, moving Shanna closer still to Kyle. Dark thighs closed over his blonde head and his tongue delved into her pussy.

The ring of bodies writhed as we used our mouths on each other. We hit the wall gently and rolled along it. First to come would break the circle. I was determined it wouldn't be me, despite the feel of cold lubricant and probing fingers in my arse as Marc prepared me.

With a cry and a shudder that transmitted around the ring Yuki came. She let go of Kyle and the ring broke. I didn't want to relinquish Olaf's big dick, but he was twirling Yuki around to impale her on it. With one last kiss of the tip I pushed away. Even dazed from orgasm Yuki managed to reach down and guide Olaf into her. She pulled her legs up to her chest, incredibly supple, and he started twirling her around his hard on like he was screwing a bolt into her. She started moaning with a second orgasm almost immediately.

Marc had two fingers up my arse, pushing away in a gentle rhythm whilst he held my erection and licked my perineum and balls. I was tempted to let him carry on until I came, but that seemed selfish. I signalled my bot over and unhooked the stirrup. Because he was shorter I twisted two of the foot loops around to be on the other side of the bar from the rest. This would bring him up to my height and let him thrust his full length into me. Even this simple job was hard because of the pleasure his fingers and tongue were giving me. I reached down, took the hand from my cock and passed the stirrup to him.

Marc understood immediately. He hooked the fingers in my back passage, pushing hard on my prostate and making me gasp, and used them as his hold as he moved around. He hooked my feet into the stirrup then started moving up my body. His free hand grabbed at my shoulder as he lined himself up. His fingers didn't pull out until he was ready to press home his erection. It slid easily into me, lubricated as I was. He kissed the back of my neck as he began gently thrusting.

We were rotating gently across the Heart toward Shanna and Kyle, who were forming a cross as they both held their stirrup and pushed back and forth on it. They spotted us coming toward them and started plotting ways to dock with us. My hard on was the biggest it's ever been. It felt like it was straining to pull away from me toward the naked bodies ahead. They let their stirrup go and strained to catch ours as we passed them.

Shanna and Kyle scissored together around us. He came up on my side, taking the head of my penis into his mouth. Shanna wrapped her arms around Marc and my waists and started rimming Marc. With her legs wrapped around Kyle she managed to keep him in her through this manoeuvre. Marc started moving in time to the tongue licking his arsehole, Kyle sucked up and down my hard on in the same rhythm.

Marc released my shoulders, staying connected to me where he was firmly wedged in my arse. I looked up to see Yuki and Olaf heading towards us. Her legs were spread wide as she aimed to land her pussy squarely on his tongue. Olaf held her, helping her aim, his dick coming back to my mouth. I caught him and swallowed his massive hard on, taking it deeper than I ever had before.

I was in ecstasy. A dick in my mouth and arse and a warm mouth around my own hard on. It wouldn't be long until I came. Marc beat me to it, pumping warm liquid deep into me. This set me off and I came in Kyle's mouth. He tried to swallow it all, but some still escaped. I reached up and started moving Olaf back and forth, making him fuck my mouth. He came all over my tongue, flooding my mouth with salty liquid. Shanna was coming, I could feel the vibrations transmitted through Kyle. Yuki was crying out in ecstasy as Marc worked his tongue in her.

We drifted apart, sated for the moment. Marc was still hard in me, but Yuki wanted his dick in her arse and mine in her pussy, or so she told us as she drifted over. Olaf, Kyle and Shanna liked that idea, and they moved together to do the same. We had hours before our rest period, and there would be plenty more combinations to try out as we got to know each other intimately.

Game Night

My new flat is near the centre of town, close to the Gay Village. So I'd started checking out some of the bars. I wasn't sure what I was hoping for, I was still too shy to go and talk to any of the other men there. I just hoped that being there would make something happen. And after a couple of weeks, it did.

It was a slow Thursday night, there weren't many people in the bar and they all looked vaguely familiar. The only one who was by himself looked away nervously when I glanced in his direction. I normally saw him with a very pretty, tall slim blonde. I wondered where she was this night, but only in passing before returning to my beer. They had one good hand pulled ale amongst all the trendy bottled lagers and I was going to savour my pint then head back to the flat.

Someone sat on the stool beside me. I looked around to see the guy I'd spotted earlier. He was younger than me, quite handsome with a square face, short, spiky dark hair and blue eyes. "Hi." he smiled.

"Hi."

"I think we're neighbours. I'm Julian." He had a very cultured accent, probably the product of an expensive school. He offered me his hand and I shook it. "Miranda and I have seen you coming and going from the apartment building."

"Miranda?"

"My wife." The blonde, at a guess.

"I'm on the first floor."

"We're on the third. We, er, we wondered if you might like to come up and......"

"And?"

"Erm, fool around." Julian had gone a bright red.

"With whom?"

"With both of us. Hopefully."

I didn't need to think long about the offer. "I'd like that. Now?"

"Yes please. Erm, just one second" Julian waved to the very camp head barman, who walked over with a big grin. Julian gave him a twenty pound note. The barman winked at me as he stuffed the note into his shirt pocket.

As we left the bar Julian told me, "Martin claimed he can tell which way someone swings after they've bought a few drinks from him. He pointed you out as a bi guy who'd like to play and bet us twenty pounds on it."

"That's an interesting skill to have."

As we got closer to the apartment building Julian became more and more nervous. When we got into the lift he admitted, "I've... We've never done this before."

"I have. Though it was more planned. It takes a lot of guts to walk up to someone in a bar and ask what you did."

Julian went bright red again. It was quite endearing. "Thanks. Maybe you can tell us what to do next."

We got off on the third floor and only had to step across the corridor from the lift to the door of Julian's flat. The door opened into the living room. The blonde, Miranda, was sat cross-legged on a big sofa playing a racing game. She dropped the controller and jumped up as we entered. "He came!" She was almost bouncing on the spot with excitement

"Martin was right, all we had to do was ask. This is......" Julian flushed again. "Robert."

"Robert thought our offer was very interesting."

We stood around for a moment, before Miranda perked up and asked, "Would you like some wine? White? Red?"

"White please."

When Miranda returned and handed out wine glasses the uncomfortable silence returned. "How should we do this?" Julian asked eventually.

I didn't really know, but I got an idea when I looked at the game on the television screen. "How about we strip race."

"Strip race?"

"I've got that game, you can have two player races. The winner stays on and the loser removes an item of clothing."

Julian and Miranda considered the idea for a moment before saying "Okay" practically together. "You boys race first." Miranda suggested.

I hadn't played the game in a while, and lost my first race to Julian. I took off my shoes and socks- voted one item- and shuffled up to let Miranda onto the sofa. Barefoot, when she lost she took off her top to reveal her bra. I tried not to stare as I took on Julian.

I did better than our first race, but still lost my T-shirt.

Miranda managed to beat her husband in the next race and he removed his footwear. I had decided I really wanted to see her breasts and was ready to do whatever it took. In the penultimate corner of the race I was close enough to her car for the plan to work. I didn't brake, instead I used her car to slow me down pushing it off the track as I did. "Cheat!" she proclaimed as her car spun on the grass. But she quickly unhooked her bra and dropped it to the floor as I crossed the finishing line. Her breasts were as good as I'd hoped. Small and firm, with very hard nipples. Julian brushed her left breast as he reached for the controller and she let out a little sigh.

Julian beat me in the next race and I was down to my boxer shorts. They both stared at the tent in my underwear before starting the next race. Miranda beat Julian and he took off his shirt. I planned to get Miranda's jeans in the next race, using the same tactic as before. But she was wise to it this time, braked very hard going into a corner and side-swiped me off the road. "Cheat." I pouted as she grinned. When her car crossed the finishing line far ahead of me I stood and pulled off my boxers.

They both stared at my erection. Then they looked at each other, grinning. Julian grabbed the controller and went through the pre race set up at record speed. However, he lost and had to remove his trousers. I was pleased to find he was commando, and we were now both naked. His dick was as hard as mine. It was slightly longer, but not as thick. Miranda took the controller off him and gave it to me.

With a naked man on either side of her, Miranda couldn't concentrate on her race, particularly as her husband brushed her breasts as he pointed out directions to her. She stood before us and slid out of her jeans, revealing a white thong. "Hold on. You're both naked. What are you going to do as a forfeit when the race is over"

I considered this. "Well, the loser could go down on the winner, I guess." I looked at Julian to see what he thought of this. He was bright red again, but he nodded with a smile.

Miranda sat on the floor facing us, watching us as we jostled each other as we raced. To be honest, I wanted to just lean over and take Julian's lovely dick into my mouth right away. But I thought about how good it would be if he were to do that to me instead and vowed to race for my blow-job. It didn't work. I kept looking down and seeing Miranda's breasts with their hard nipples. I spun off half way through the second lap and couldn't possibly win. I handed the controller to Miranda. "What's this for?"

"Well, you've got to race him whilst I do my forfeit." I knelt before Julian and spread his legs so I could get at his magnificent hard on. I licked the under side of it and he almost crashed as he looked down at me. "Finish your winning lap." I told him. He nodded, but I could imagine how hard it was for him to concentrate as I swirled my tongue around the red head of his dick.

I slowed down my sucking when Julian had finished, to let him set up the next race, then I took a ball into my mouth just as it started. Julian was all over the track. Miranda giggled and pulled away for an early lead. My tactic was to distract Julian as much as possible and make him lose, but Miranda was too busy looking down at what I was doing to draw her lead out very far. I opened my mouth and took as much as I could of Julian's dick into it before closing my lips around the shaft and drawing back up with a slurp. At that point it was obvious that Julian wasn't going to win the race. I pooled saliva in my mouth to lubricate as I began bobbing my head up and down. Julian let the controller drop to the seat and leaned back against the cushion. Miranda did a parade lap to win then set her controller aside.

"What's my forfeit?" Julian asked.

I finally let his dick out of my mouth to tell him "That's for Miranda to decide." As she thought about this I cupped his balls with my left hand and gently jacked him off with my right. He squirmed on the seat, sliding further and further off it.

"I want you two to suck each other." Miranda announced, "Do a 69."

I shuffled away from the sofa and lay on my side on the floor. Julian came over and laid down so that his penis was level with my face and I could feel his warm breath on my crotch. I took his hard on in my hand and kissed the head. He did the same to me. I licked the under side of his dick and he licked mine.

As Julian became more confident he stopped following my lead and tried out things for himself. He took me in his mouth and swirled his tongue around the shaft. I licked his balls then moved my tongue up one side then the other.

Miranda sat beside me and kissed her way up my body. When she reached my head I offered her her husband's dick and she sucked eagerly on it before kissing her way up his body. When she got to Julian's head he offered her my hard on and they licked and kissed it together.

As I bobbed my head up and down on the top of Julian's shaft he stopped licking me and started groaning. He was about to come. Miranda rushed round and started sucking his balls and licking the base of his dick. I felt the spasms as he start pumping come then tasted it as it hit my tongue. There was a lot of it. I swallowed what I could but some escaped from the sides of my mouth. Then I pulled the still spurting penis from my mouth and Miranda took it in hers and sucked up the last of the come.

Julian and I rolled onto our backs away from each other. I brushed some sticky semen from around my mouth and licked it off my fingers. Miranda moved down and I soon felt her mouth on my cock head. She licked it up and down then took it as deep into her mouth as she could. I let out a satisfied groan as Julian joined his wife and took my balls in his mouth.

They started passing my hard on back and forth. First one would suck the head and lick around it whilst the other licked the base of the shaft and the balls, then they'd change. It wasn't long before I came. They both fought each other with their tongues to get the most of my spunk.

I was still hard after I'd come. Miranda was eyeing my erection. "Honey. Can I?" she asked Julian.

"I want to see that."

"Can you get the box."

As Julian went into the bedroom Miranda stretched out on the floor and beckoned me over. I tugged her thong downward, revealing shaved pubes and a pink, wet pussy. I spread Miranda's thighs and kissed around her crotch. When Julian returned he found me licking up and down her slit. I stopped just long enough to suggest, "Why don't you lube up my arse." He dug in the little wooden box and pulled out a tube of lube. He passed me a condom and unscrewed the tube.

I rolled the condom down my shaft and moved up Miranda's body. Julian reached down and helped guide me into his wife. Miranda moaned as I slid easily into her very wet pussy. When I was buried as deep as I'd go in her she hooked her legs around my thighs and reached back to pull my butt cheeks apart.

Something cold ran down my crack and pooled at my sphincter. Something pushed at my hole and I relaxed it. Julian's finger slid into me. Then it pulled out and more lube was squirted into the hole. I pulled out of Miranda, pushing back onto the finger, then thrust back into her slowly. When I pulled out again Julian managed to get two fingers into me.

I stayed still and Julian started pumping my arse with his fingers. He rocked me back and forth and I ground against Miranda. She kissed all around my face and made little moans.

Julian pulled his fingers out of me and squirted more lube into me. Then he leaned back to get a condom and roll it onto his hard on. "Oh yes." Miranda sighed, "Put it into him."

Julian placed his hard on against my arsehole and started pushing. I tried to relax and let him in. I've played with my arse with my fingers and toys, but nothing is quite as satisfying as a good hard dick. As it eased through my ring I began to shiver with pleasure.

As Julian buried himself in me Miranda held me tight. As he started pushing in and out of me I moved under him, grinding against her clit. She came loudly, calling out to her husband to thrust harder. Then, as I came and filled the condom, she came again. Julian thrust a few more times then sighed as he came as well.

We slid gently out of each other and laid in a tangle on the floor. "Wow." said Julian.

"I told you this would be great." said Miranda, kissing her husband. Then she kissed me, "Thank you for joining our fantasy."

"Will you come to bed with us?" Julian asked, "We don't have to go to work tomorrow so...."

"I work from home, so I can get up when I want." I told him, "Id love to go to bed with you." I got up, slightly shakily, and picked up the box.

Julian and Miranda stood either side of me and put their arms around my waist. "We should have games nights every week or so." Miranda suggested, "Maybe we can get Martin to suggest a girl for me."

Capture The Flag

Eve eyed the row of little figures on the edge of the table. She had dropped down to their level to get a better view. "Did you paint these?" she asked Dave.

"We both did." Rebecca answered, "I did that one, that one and...... that one. And all of mine." She proudly pointed at the figures in front of her.

They were sat around a large oval dining table. Dave had his own set of figures in front of his seat. He was busy laying out landscape and buildings "We're going to set up a production line some time, do whole armies at once."

Eve took the pad and pen Rebecca offered her. "Is this going to turn me into a geek?" she asked.

"If you're lucky, yes." There was something cheeky, almost suggestive, about Rebecca's smile. In her own home she was quite different from the businesslike co-worker Eve knew. Her hair was cut short, in a way that perfectly suited her small round face. She wore a tight white T-shirt and cut off denim shorts and was barefoot. Eve had the impression that this off duty Rebecca could be very naughty. A thrill ran through her body, her nipples tautened and the tops of her thighs suddenly felt very warm. It had been a long time since she had had thoughts like that about another woman. She took the pad and unconsciously covered her chest from view with it.

"This is our Sunday hangover cure. It gets the brain working again."

"I don't think it's fair that you two already know the rules."

"We'll be gentle with you. And we'll explain everything as it comes up."

"Including the special rules." Rebecca chipped in. Dave looked surprised at this. They shared a quick glance. "If they come up." Rebecca added.

"Okay. So what is the aim of the game."

"We'll do a simple capture the flag. To the deaths can take ages. Especially when the special rules are being used. You have to get one or more of your team into this building here," Dave pointed at a structure in the middle of the table, "and capture the token that's in there. Then you have to get the token back to your own base. All the time we will be trying to do the same, as well as flanking around to cut off each others' escape routes and steal the token back if we can. Bear in mind that the character with the token can't use their weapons, so you may want to give that job to whichever has the weakest weapons. You've got the cards which tell you speeds, strength etcetera. The rest will become obvious as we play."

Eve nodded. She wasn't sure this was going to help her hangover in the slightest. But she had to admit, she was intrigued, and Dave and Rebecca were good company. They'd been very understanding the night before when she got very drunk and went on about her break up with Martin. She could see this being fun, in its own geeky way, and far better than the moping and feeling sorry for herself she would have been doing at home. "Okay then. Let battle commence." she declared.

Eve didn't really think about tactics, she just had all her figures rush for the structure. Surely they'd stand a better chance in a fight if they were all together. Rebecca and Dave seemed to be doing the same. As they drew closer, however, they began spreading out, coming around the building rather than entering it. Eve sent her thief in for the token and tried to arrange the others for defence.

Rebecca and Dave sent characters after the token as well. Bigger, meaner characters. Eve's small and weak thief was caught by four barbarians and run through in a couple of conclusive dice rolls. "Are you teaming up against me?" she pouted.

"No. Not really. Now we get to fight each other for the token." Dave admitted.

"It's a shame about the thief," Eve sighed, "I was going to have him run away with the token whilst the rest of my team kept you busy."

"Well there is a special rule." Rebecca offered. "You can resurrect him if you want."

"Really? How?"

"Well, the way we play it is a forfeit. Swap a piece of clothing for your character back."

"You play this as a strip game?"

"It certainly takes our minds off the hangover." Dave said with a smile. "Of course we don't have to if...."

Before he'd even finished, Eve was pulling her T-shirt off. She wasn't sure why she did it, the only explanation she could come up with was that she wanted to see what happened next. Her only regret was that she was wearing a plain bra. Dave looked surprised, but happy. Rebecca smiled. "Where can I put him?"

"Back with the rest of your team, I guess." Dave moved the figure back to its team mates.

Across the table, the nipples on Rebecca's tiny tits stood out, pressing against the material of her T-shirt. Eve knew what her next tactic was going to be. She turned her gang towards the structure, trapping Rebecca's two barbarians between her full force and Dave's barbarians. Rebecca's smile actually got bigger.

Tactics went out of the window as everyone stormed into the building. Rebecca's barbarians put up a spirited defence, but they fell at the same time. Eve looked at her across the table and raised her eyebrows questioningly. "We'll wait until the end of the round and then settle up." Dave said, "I reckon there'll be a few more deaths before we're done."

There were several more deaths. One of Dave's barbarians also fell under the onslaught, and Eve lost two of her team. Rebecca's thief blundered into the building and was quickly despatched. "That's a lot of resurrections." Eve smiled. "Who wants to go first?"

Rebecca stood and pulled off her T-shirt. She wasn't wearing a bra. Eve grinned at the tiny tits with their prominent stiff nipples. She grinned even more as Rebecca slid the cut offs down her legs and revealed she wore no knickers. Her pubic hair was trimmed neatly above prominent puffy labia lips. Eve could feel herself heating up just looking. She slipped off her bra and pulled down her jeans. Dave pulled his T-shirt off and tossed it aside. He turned to his girlfriend, "Didn't you lose three fighters? That was only two pieces of clothing."

"I need to do another forfeit?"

"Yes. What could it possibly be?" Dave looked across at Eve, who had flushed. She knew exactly what she wanted Rebecca to do, but she couldn't seem to make the words form. "Why don't you give Eve a kiss?" Dave said for her.

Rebecca walked around the table to Eve, who slid her chair back. Rebecca straddled Eve's legs and leaned in. She had to support herself with a hand on Eve's shoulder. The first kiss was a tease, lips just brushing, but enough to get Eve's heart racing and a flush across her breasts. Rebecca's free hand slipped down to brush Eve's left breast, teasing the nipple up to a point and then tweaking it. Eve gasped, and Rebecca dived in. Their lips locked and Rebecca's tongue probed the inside of Eve's mouth.

Eve moved her hands up, nervously reaching out to touch Rebecca's thighs. Her left hand traced past Rebecca's waist all the way up to cup a small breast. Her right hand made its way up Rebecca's inner thigh, drawn to the heat emanating from the pussy above. Rebecca squirmed as first one then two fingers slid in. As she felt the slippery enveloping warmth clasp her probing fingers Eve wondered why it had been so long since she had last made love with a woman. And why she had let herself get seduced by strip role playing. Then her fingers were all the way inside Rebecca and she knew why she was doing this. Because it felt right. These two were nothing like the selfish stuck up prick who'd dumped her. They were much more fun, much more interesting.

Rebecca was moving on Eve's fingers, up and down and occasionally back and forth. Just when Eve thought she was going to push her colleague over the edge, Rebecca stopped. She eased Eve's fingers out of her pussy and, unsteadily, stood up. "Time for the next round." she announced. Before going back to her seat she took Eve's hand and sucked both the fingers that had been giving her so much pleasure, licking them clean of her juices. Eve almost melted.

Somehow Eve managed to move her chair back to the table. She looked across at Dave and realised that he had been watching all the time she'd been finger fucking his girlfriend. His presence didn't bother her in the slightest. "How many of your men do I have to kill before you're naked?" she asked him.

"Only the one."

Eve looked across at Rebecca, flushed but back in her seat and ready to continue fighting. They both smiled. The next round's tactics were obvious. They both attacked Dave's team, but somehow only managed to kill one of them. Meanwhile Eve lost another two of her fighters. Dave stood, and the tent in his climbing trousers made it obvious how excited he was. He pushed the trousers down past the erection that tried to hook into the waistband.

Eve couldn't help but stare. Martin's cock had been tiny, even when fully erect. Dave's was at least twice the length, and much, much thicker, than her ex boyfriend's. "You lucky girl." she said to Rebecca without taking her eyes off the hard on.

Rebecca brought her chair around the table and sat beside Eve. "Your forfeits." Eve nodded and stood to pull her knickers off. Her pubic hair was shaggy compared to Rebecca's neatly trimmed bush, and she nervously ran fingers through it.

"What's my forfeit going to be?" Eve asked, shivering with nervous excitement as Dave and Rebecca stared at her.

"Your forfeit is to tell us exactly what you want to do. And we will do it."

Dave had come to stand on Eve's left. She looked down at his big hard on, wanting to reach down and touch it. So she did, pulling the foreskin back to reveal the deep red head and stroking it gently. "I want this beautiful thing in me. I want to go down on you whilst Dave fucks me."

Rebecca smiled and, taking Eve's hand, led her to the bedroom. Eve didn't let go of Dave's cock, bringing him with them. She released him when they stood before the double bed and Rebecca turned to kiss her. Their hands stroked over each other's bodies as Eve gently eased Rebecca toward the bed.

Rebecca dropped onto the bed and crawled backwards up it. She sat back on the pillows, spread her legs and beckoned Eve toward her. Eve jumped onto the bed and placed herself between Rebecca's legs. She glanced over at Dave, who was unrolling a condom onto his hard on, then dived for Rebecca's pussy. She wanted to taste it. It had been so long since she had savoured the sharp taste of another woman. Her tongue teased at Rebecca's puffy lips then licked along their length, splitting them.

Rebecca's labia pouted open and glistening before Eve. She felt the bed shift as Dave climbed onto it and she spread her legs wider as she dipped her mouth to Rebecca's pussy again. She found, and pressed her tongue hard against, Rebecca's clitoris as a large warm cock head eased gently through the entrance to her own vagina. With her tongue pressed flat against the hard nub she felt herself being pushed against it as Dave slid into her. She hadn't realised just how excited she was until she took Dave's length and girth with ease.

It felt so good to be filled again. After two years of Martin's tiny prick Dave's cock was a revelation. Her moan vibrated against Rebecca's clit. Rebecca reached down and ran fingers through Eve's hair, encouraging her to move her head from side to side as well as back and forth. Dave began slowly pulling out. Eve's body tried to follow him, and keep her tongue in contact with Rebecca's nub at the same time. She had to admit defeat and let him slide almost all the way out of her.

Then Dave thrust back in, and Eve's tongue was crushed against Rebecca's lips and clitoris. She grasped Eve's hair and held her in place as Dave pulled out again. Eve couldn't believe how controlled Dave was with his long, slow, strong thrusts. She was right on the edge of orgasm, and she could feel Rebecca beginning to shiver and shake with impending climax.

Eve hooked her tongue, squeezing it between Rebecca's pussy lips and then moving it up to lick the whole length of the slit as Dave pulled out of her. Rebecca squealed with joy and began shaking beneath her, legs clasping her shoulders and holding her tight as she rode out the orgasm.

Dave had paused in his thrusts, probably to enjoy the show. Now he started moving again, still making those long, controlled strokes. Eve arched her back and straightened her arms, changing Dave's angle so he pressed against the front wall of her vagina. She stared down at Rebecca, holding her gaze and sharing the joy. Rebecca smiled at her and slowly sat up to kiss her. She licked her own juices off Eve's lips and reached down to play with her firm breasts and taut nipples.

Eve's breath was coming in sobs as she reached the edge. Rebecca held her tight as she started making short cries as fast as she could draw breath. They toppled forward as Eve's arms gave way. She hugged Rebecca close and shook with joy as tears of pleasure rolled down her cheeks. Dave had followed her down, staying inside her, but now he pulled out gently and laid beside her, hugging her from the opposite side to Rebecca.

Rebecca wiped the tears from Eve's cheeks and kissed her earlobe. Eve sighed, "Well, that did cure my hangover."

"It usually does." Rebecca whispered.

They both looked down at Dave's still hard, and still impressive, erection. "You didn't come?" Rebecca asked.

"Oh he will." Eve told her. "I want to see you ride him. And whilst you do that, I think I'm going to sit on his face."

Rebecca grinned and clambered over Eve in her eagerness to get at her boyfriend's dick. She grabbed it, swung her leg over him and then sank onto it in one smooth move.

Eve kissed her way up Rebecca's thigh then her body, pausing to give special attention to her breasts. She swung her leg over Dave's head, looking down to check her pussy was right over his waiting lips. He sneaked his tongue out and flicked at her engorged labia and she squeaked and jumped. When she sank back down she was ready for the tongue and merely squirmed, trying to find a good position.

Rebecca rested her hands on Eve's shoulders, and used the hold to balance as she moved up and down Dave's cock. She moaned every time she sank all the way down and kissed Eve when she was at the top of her stroke. Eve reached out and tweaked Rebecca's nipples, which drove the smaller woman to move faster. Soon Rebecca was moving too quickly for Eve to keep hold of her. Dave's tongue working hard between her hot pussy lips wasn't making it easy to concentrate either.

Eve came. She toppled over, off Dave's face, grasping at her hot and wet vagina. As she squeezed her hands between her thighs Rebecca and Dave paused to look down at her. She beamed, "Don't stop."

Rebecca leant on Dave's chest and levered her arse up and down, pumping Dave's hard on in and out of her faster and faster. Eve reached out and smacked Rebecca's tight little buttocks lightly. Dave was thrusting up on each of Rebecca's down strokes, as best he could. They were both close to coming. Eve moved in close to watch Rebecca's pussy lips pouting around Dave's cock as it pulled out and pursing around it as it pushed in. She wanted to reach in and touch the point where they met, but knew better than to put them off so close to climax.

Rebecca came, but kept on pumping her arse up and down, prolonging the pleasure. Dave kept on thrusting for a few moments more, until he too came. Rebecca snuggled her small frame on his chest and they both grinned at Eve. She cuddled up to them. "How did you know? That I'd do this?"

"We didn't." Rebecca admitted. "But you told us last night that you're bi, and you complained about that little shit of an ex boyfriend. I just guessed you'd want to, y'know. And when you accepted the first special rule I was sure you'd be up for it."

"I just played along. I wasn't sure Becca would even go through with it." Dave admitted.

"You played well." Eve rubbed against her two new lovers. "Much more of this and maybe you will make me a geek."

Morning Glory

Mike woke to soft lips nibbling at his neck and earlobe. He sighed and stirred.

"I thought that would get you up." whispered Karen in his ear, "Now to get this up." She threw the covers back and reached down to gently stroke his rising penis, giggling as it twitched and grew with each caress. "Very nice." she commented, "But I think I deserve some attention now."

Karen moved quickly, scooting up to straddle Mike's head and offer her pussy to his mouth. She braced herself against the wall as his tongue started licking along the slit, parting the lips and exploring deeper. "That's it, get me wet. Get me ready for your cock."

Mike cupped Karen's butt cheeks, using them to move her around. After a bit of exploration they clenched tight and she resisted his guiding hands. He had found just the right spot. Mike ground his tongue against her clitoris as she made appreciative whimpers.

There was the clink of crockery on a tray, then a sigh and theatrical tutting as Roger pretended to be shocked at what he had found when he walked back into the bedroom. "Well, I went away to make coffee and you two started without me. That's not very polite."

"Darling I was just priming Mike for you. Look at that cock, you know what it wants."

Mike couldn't see Roger, but he heard the tray being put down and felt the mattress shift as someone joined them in bed. Then he felt a tongue lick along the underside of his hard on and fingers lift it to a warm and eager mouth. Karen lowered herself and ground even harder against Mike's tongue, turned on by what her boyfriend was doing to him.

Karen was right on the edge of an orgasm, but she decided she wanted to be pushed over by something other than Mike's tongue. "Condom." she sighed. Roger knew exactly what she meant. His lips moved from Mike's shaft and he moved off the bed again. He knew exactly where Mike kept his condoms and had one out of its wrapper in no time. With a last kiss of Mike's dark red cock head he began rolling the sheath on.

When the condom was fully fitted Roger stood beside Karen and kissed her passionately. "That's a very skilled mouth," she said when they parted, "don't let it go to waste." She shuffled down Mike's body and placed herself over his cock. Her serious expression as she guided it into herself was replaced by a triumphant smile as she took it all in.

Roger was wearing boxer shorts, but they were impressively tented out. As he removed the shorts to reveal his fat hard on Mike reached out to grab it and draw it toward his mouth. With his other hand he reached up and cupped one of Karen's small breasts, stroking it then pinching the nipple. She began moving up and down his shaft, the orgasm building again.

Roger had to climb onto the bed again so Mike could lick along the underside of his cock then kiss and play with his balls. Then he twisted his head to the side and took as much of Roger's dick as he could into his mouth. Roger leaned over to Karen and they kissed again.

They set up a rhythm, Mike moving his head back and forth and running his tongue over Roger's cock head, Karen sliding up and down Mike's shaft and Roger trying to keep still but steal kisses from Karen. Soon enough, though, Karen buried Mike deep in herself as she cried out in orgasm. As she sank forward to rest on Mike's chest it was obvious this stage of the lovemaking was over.

After a moment's rest Karen pulled herself off Mike and went to stand behind Roger. "Your turn." she said.

"I'm going to need a little lube." Roger told her. The comment was redundant as she already had the tube out of the bedside drawer and was squirting glistening liquid onto her fingers.

Mike teased Roger's cock with light flicks of his tongue along the shaft. Under this teasing, and with Karen pushing lubricant into his arse, Roger trembled as he tried to keep still. Mike wanted Roger to come, to spurt into his mouth, but he also wanted Roger sat on his cock. He held back on pushing Roger over the edge

Satisfied with her work on Roger's arse, Karen moved her attention to Mike's cock, still hard and glistening with her juices. She held it up, added a swirl of lubricant and smiled.

Mike gave Roger's cock one last kiss and let it go. Roger moved down the bed and swung himself over Mike. Karen helped line up Mike's hard on with Roger's hole and urged her boyfriend on as he sank down on it. Karen had been tight, but this was tighter. Roger relaxed and pushed down. After a little more easing Mike's cock head pushed gently past the barrier of Roger's sphincter, causing them both to give a little cry of triumph.

Roger sank all the way down Mike's shaft and rested there for a moment. His own still hard cock twitched. Karen pressed herself against his back and reached round to play with the hard on. Stroking it in time she began grinding against Roger. He took up the rhythm and started moving up and down. Mike laid back and enjoyed the show and the sensations.

All too soon Mike came. As Roger's sphincter muscles massaged his shaft, Mike filled the condom. Roger sat back and groaned as Karen's hand moved faster on his shaft. With her urging he came all over Mike's chest. The three of them collapsed together in a sticky, satisfied huddle. When they had caught their breath Karen slid down to lie beside Mike and Roger gently lifted himself off Mike's cock to lie the other side of her.

"You two should visit more often." Mike told them "Did you say something about coffee?"

I Have Never

Drinking games can be a terrible waste of drinking time. Late on a Friday night, however, Mark wasn't bothered about slowing down. And "I Have Never" was always fun for the occasional revelation. It was a mixed bunch around the table, and it hadn't yet dipped into cheeky dredging up of old embarrassments.

"I have never," announced Jill, "had sex with a woman." All the men at the table took a drink.

Clockwise around the table was Steve, Jill's boyfriend. He smirked and came back with the only possible follow on, "I have never had sex with a man." The three women at the table, and Mark, took a drink.

Mark found himself being stared at. "No." said Jill, "Really."

"Really. Well strictly speaking it was a man and his wife."

"At the same time?"

"At the same time."

The game was derailed for a while, the next person around the table was stumped for anything to say. Across the table from Mark a young man he didn't really know- Paul- had gone an endearing shade of red. He smiled and took another drink before waiting for a revelation.

The night wound down and the pub eventually threw them out. Everyone went their separate ways and Mark found himself walking down the leafy streets with Paul. After a while the younger man asked, "What's it like with another man?"

"It was fun. Very hot. It was part of a threesome, so it couldn't be anything else."

"Did you do...... everything?"

"No. I only gave him a blow job. But oral sex is still sex." Mark looked across at Paul. It was hard to tell under the street lights, but the boy appeared to be blushing again. He was blonde and twinky, quite pretty in the way that Mark had always known he'd go for. "Do you think about sex with another man."

Paul nodded, "Quite a lot. I'm a crap bisexual, I can't get it on with a man."

They both lived on the same street, Paul at the opposite end to Mark. As they neared Mark's house he decided to take a risk. "Do you want to? We could, y'know...." Now it was his turn to blush.

"Okay."

As they climbed the stairs to Mark's flat his heart started beating far harder than the exercise merited. He hadn't so easily and casually got himself into a situation where sex was imminent ever before. Whatever came next was going to be all new.

When he had closed the flat door they stood in the small hallway for a while. "Do you want a whisky?" Mark asked.

"Please." Paul croaked.

When Mark returned from the kitchen with two large measures of whisky Paul was still standing in the hallway. "Lets go into the living room." Mark suggested.

They sat side by side on the sofa. Paul swirled his whisky around the glass. "So, er, what do we do now?" he asked.

Mark knocked back the rest of his whisky and put the glass aside. "Well, if you're sure about this." Paul nodded. Mark slid off the sofa and placed himself on the floor before the younger man. "Sit back."

Paul made himself comfortable against the cushions of the sofa. His breathing had sped up as he stared down at Mark. He too drained his whisky and put it aside. They looked at each other for a moment, then Paul gave the slightest of nods. Mark smiled. He reached up, pushed Paul's T-shirt up and released his belt.

Carefully, trying to hide the nervous tremble in his hands, Mark undid the buttons on Paul's jeans one by one. By the time he had reached the last one he could feel the warmth and solidity of what lay beneath the black boxers. "Lift up." he suggested. Paul raised himself slightly off the seat so that Mark could pull the jeans and boxers all the way down his legs.

Mark's gaze had followed the clothing down to Paul's feet as he had pulled and pushed it down, so he didn't see the prize he'd uncovered until he looked up again. Paul's cock was slim and pale, rather like its owner. It lay along Paul's right leg, twitching and growing as Mark stared at it. The erection grew and stood up, the foreskin pulling back to reveal a deep red head.

Mark spread Paul's legs so he could move closer. He move a finger up one side of the hard on and back down the other. Paul shivered. Mark moved in close, so he could feel the warmth of the erection against his cheek. He nibbled with his lips from the hair at the base all the way to the tip. Here he flicked out his tongue and swirled around the head of Paul's cock.

Mark licked his lips and pooled saliva in his mouth. With fingers wrapped halfway down Paul's cock he dipped to swallow the head and as much of it as he could take. Paul sighed and squirmed. Mark slurped up and down the dick, taking in a little more each time. He stopped with just the head in his mouth, feeling it twitch against his tongue.

Paul was staring at what Mark was doing. He bit his lip and shifted slightly. When Mark released his hard on Paul made an involuntary little noise. Mark smiled. He reached down and gently lifted Paul's balls so he could kiss them and, very gently, suck them. Then he licked Paul's cock from base to tip and back again. Paul threw his head back and grasped the cushions on the sofa.

Teasing Paul, Mark licked all around his cock, flicking at the head as it twitched. Then he dived back to sucking it again. With the head in his mouth he swirled his tongue around it and started sucking up and down again.

Paul grasped Mark's shoulder. "Gonna come." Mark nodded, but carried on sucking. Paul's cock started twitching as it pumped semen up its length. Mark drew it out until the head was only just in his mouth, so the clammy liquid landed on his tongue. Paul's cock was still pumping out little drops of come when Mark let it slip from his lips. He swirled the semen around his mouth and swallowed it. Then he licked a drop from the tip of Paul's still hard cock. Paul jumped and made a little hiss.

Mark sat back and looked at Paul, who had sprawled back on the sofa. He adjusted his own hard on, which was rock solid. Paul spotted this and sat up. "Take your clothes off." he demanded.

Mark stood before Paul and unfastened his belt. The younger man slid off the sofa to kneel, reaching up and pulling Mark's trousers down as soon as they were unfastened. Mark's erection was straining at his boxers. Paul stroked it through the material. He teased it until the head pushed under the waistband, then tugged the boxers down.

Shuffling forward Paul got himself into position so Mark's cock was level with his face. It was thicker and darker than his, and just a little bit longer. He wanted to do something with it, but he wasn't quite sure what. With one hand on Mark's thigh Paul reached out and gently drew the erection toward his mouth. He kissed the head, then some of the way down the shaft, then he tried licking it. He obviously enjoyed the taste, because once he had started he couldn't stop.

Mark pulled his shirt and T-shirt off and stared down at the young man who was using his erection to learn how to give blow jobs. The thought amused him, and turned him on more. He decided to let Paul work out for himself what he should do. But that wasn't going to be easy. Mark clasped his hands behind his back to keep from reaching out and guiding the student.

Paul tried to remember what had turned him on about blow jobs he'd been given. What had been the best thing about Mark going down on him? All of it, he thought, which didn't really help him decide what to do next. But then it was obvious what he should do next. He hadn't yet taken Mark's hard on into his mouth. He moved, lifted up a little, and then closed his lips around the warm red head.

"Oh yeah." Mark moaned. Paul smiled, he was doing something right. He moved to take more of the cock into his mouth. With every little bit more that Paul swallowed, Mark made another appreciative noise. Eventually he'd taken as much as he could of the erection into his mouth. Before he started gagging he drew back all the way to the head. This raised another moan. So long as he didn't bite there was little he could do wrong.

Letting Paul explore and work things out for himself had been a great idea, Mark decided. He had a wonderful tingling feeling in his scrotum as his balls drew back. A warm and playful mouth and tongue were driving him ever closer to the edge. It wouldn't be long now. "Gonna..."

Paul looked up, Mark's cock popping out of his mouth as he did so. The first spurts of semen hit his chin and neck, then his T-shirt. Realising his mistake he clamped his mouth over the head to suck out the last of the come. He wasn't so sure about the taste, but it wasn't horrible. In a way it tasted of victory and a milestone achieved.

When he was sure no more could be sucked out of Mark's subsiding erection Paul sat back. Mark shuffled round and sat on the sofa. They were both quiet for a while.

Paul wiped the semen off his chin and neck with his T-shirt, then he pulled it off. "That's a little sticky."

"So what did you think?" Mark asked.

"It's definitely a shame I took so long to get round to doing that."

"Do you want to do it again?"

Paul's erection was growing again, but he shook his head. "Not.... Not right now. Can I borrow a T-shirt, just till I get home."

"Sure."

They both pulled their trousers up and walked through the flat bare chested. In the bedroom Mark pulled a plain black T-shirt out and handed it to Paul. "Here you go."

"Thanks. Are you doing anything tomorrow?"

"I don't have anything planned."

"I'll drop this back some time then."

Paul dressed quickly, putting his semen stained T-shirt into a bag Mark found for him. At the door he paused, "Thanks for...."

"Any time."

"See you tomorrow."

* * *

Mark woke late the next morning. He ate breakfast whilst surfing porn sites then had a shower. He was considering a lazy day lounging around the flat with just his dressing gown on when the buzzer for the door rang.

"Hello."

"I thought I'd return your T-shirt."

"Come on up." Mark pressed the button to open the building's front door and unlatched the door to the flat. When Paul entered the flat, Mark was in the kitchen watching a kettle boil. "Would you like a cup of tea?"

"Thanks."

Whilst they waited in the kitchen for the kettle to boil Mark studied the man he'd given a blow job to the night before in daylight. Paul was slightly taller than Mark, with floppy blonde hair that threatened to fall across his pretty young face. He was slim and stood at ease in the doorway to the kitchen. A lot more ease than Mark felt when he realised his cock was growing hard thinking about what they had done the night before. He worried that the front of his dressing gown would be pushed out by his hard on, giving him away. He turned to the counter to pour the water into the teapot.

Paul sat on the sofa in the living room and Mark took the chair before his computer. He carefully rearranged his dressing gown so as to show nothing off. They sipped tea in silence for a while.

"Last night was fun." Paul managed eventually, "Would you like to.... er do you want to do it again?"

"Yes." Mark worried that he sounded too eager, "All you have to do is ask. You want to....?"

Paul nodded. "But I was wondering. I wanted to ask. Have you ever done anal?"

"No." Mark managed after a moment.

"Giving or receiving?"

"No."

"I'd like you to.... Would you fuck me in the arse?"

"Okay." As Mark recovered his composure he smiled. "We'll need to get some stuff. Lube, condoms, that sort of thing. Let me get dressed and then we'll head into town."

* * *

They made small talk on the bus into town, discussing films and television. Mark led the way to a sex shop which catered to most tastes, gay, straight or bi. As they entered the door together they both became nervous. It was going to be so obvious why they were there. They felt as if the eyes of all the small number of shoppers and staff were on them.

Mark picked up a big bottle of anal lube. "You can never have too much." he whispered to Paul.

"I thought you'd never....."

"I've put toys up there." Mark picked up a box of condoms. He turned to a shelf full of butt plugs.

Paul stared at the toys. "You want one?" Mark asked.

"Er...."

"They're good for getting you used to having something up there. It'll relax you."

"Okay." Paul reached out. His hand hovered over the boxes of toys. He tried to remember how big Mark's cock had been, but ended up selecting a butt plug which was smaller. "I'll buy myself this one."

They hardly talked at all on the bus back to the flat. With their purchases in plain plastic bags they stared out of the window and hoped that no-one could guess what they were about to do. Back at the flat they put the bags down on the bed. "Do you want something to eat?" Mark asked.

"No."

"Want to have a shower?"

"Yeah."

They stood for a moment before Mark started undressing. Paul followed suit like it was a race. In under a minute they were both naked, their erections swinging up to stiffness. In unison they each reached for the other's cock and gently teased and stroked it. Before they got too carried away, Mark led the way into the bathroom.

Under the warm water Mark took the lead. He soaped Paul up and smoothed the lather over the young man's smooth skin. He had read that it was key to be relaxed before trying anal sex, and he intended to sooth Paul as much as he possibly could. Standing behind Paul, Mark pressed against his lover. His erection found a natural resting place between taut buttocks, a hint of what was to come.

Mark turned Paul around and dropped to his knees. He took the glistening wet hard on in his mouth and swirled his tongue around the head. Paul reached out to steady himself. Mark smiled around the cock then swallowed as much of it as he could. But, tease that he was, he just as quickly released it. "Ohhhh." Paul moaned.

"You ready?"

"I am so fucking ready."

"Come on then."

They dried off quickly, and Mark grabbed a spare towel on the way to the bedroom. He laid it on the bed, and Paul stretched out on it on his stomach. As Mark moved around arranging paraphernalia Paul watched him, flushing a bright red and biting his lip when the butt plug appeared.

Mark spread Paul's legs and knelt between them. Paul, barely consciously, lifted his arse up to present it better. Mark kneaded the taut buttocks. He popped the top off the tube of lube and, spreading Paul's butt cheeks with his left hand, squeezed out a little of the clear liquid around the rose of his arsehole.

Switching the hand holding the lubricant, Mark smeared his right forefinger with it. He swirled the finger through the lube around Paul's arsehole. Paul was grasping the pillow tightly, waiting, waiting for Mark's finger to enter him. Mark eased it in gently and smoothly, up to the second knuckle. He held it there for a moment, then started slowly pumping it in and out, slightly deeper each time.

Paul tilted his arse up further, lifting his cock so it only touched the towel with its tip. Mark put the tube down and played with Paul's balls for a moment. Paul made an annoyed noise when Mark pulled his finger out, then sighed as Mark snatched up the lube and spread more of it around. This time Mark squeezed two fingers into Paul, pumping them and probing for the prostate with them.

Mark reached for the butt plug, then juggled it, the lube and the fingers in Paul's arse. He wiped lube off his right hand after the plug slipped from his grip and tried again. Paul looked around, guessing what came next. After coating the butt plug with lube Mark pushed it in. Paul relaxed, as best he could, and soon the flared head popped past the ring of his sphincter. Paul loved the feeling of being filled, squirming and pumping his arse just to feel the plug move inside him.

Mark sat back and enjoyed the view. He wanted to give Paul time to get used to the butt plug, and to relax ready for a cock. He moved up the bed and presented his hard on to Paul, who grinned and reached out for it and started nuzzling around the balls. Mark let Paul lick his shaft and balls until his erection became even larger and harder. Much as he loved the attention he knew he didn't want to come from a blow job when there was a virgin arse awaiting him. He moved back down the bed and put a condom on.

With his sheathed cock lubed up and ready, Mark reached for the butt plug and started pulling it out. Paul made a little "Oh!" as the plug popped out. Mark dropped the plug to one side and quickly angled his cock to Paul's dilated sphincter. He pushed it into place with his hand, until the head lodged inside the muscle ring, then put his weight behind it.

Paul raised his arse to meet Mark's erection. They squeezed together slowly until Mark was completely buried in Paul's arse. He stretched out against the younger man's smooth skin and enjoyed the tight, warm squeezing of his cock. "Wow." said Paul beneath him.

"Wow," Mark echoed.

Paul turned his head, and Mark reached down and they kissed. For a moment that felt odder than Mark's cock head deep in Paul's arse. "Ready?" Mark asked.

"Fuck me." Paul requested.

Mark pulled out, then, gently, pushed back in. Paul sighed under him and cocked his arse up further. With each of Mark's thrusts Paul lifted himself higher off the bed. After a while they had to stop so Mark could adjust his position for better penetration. He reached around to hold Paul's hard on.

It took a few thrusts to get it right, but Mark was soon stroking it in rhythm with his movements. As he moved harder and faster, however, he lost the beat again. Grasping Paul's waist for stability, Mark began pounding Paul's arse harder and faster. Paul reached back and started masturbating himself.

With a rising crescendo of grunts and moans they headed rapidly to climax. With a final push as deep as he could go Mark filled the condom in Paul's arse. A few strokes later Paul himself came, squirting all over the towel.

Mark let Paul sink to the bed, slowly pulling his cock from the younger man's arse as he did. Paul let out a little moan as the cock head finally popped out past his sphincter. They laid side by side, for a while only able to say "Wow."

"Another shower?" Mark suggested after a while.

"Yeah. I think so." Before they got up Paul asked, "Do you want to try that? It's incredible."

"Hell yes."

Under the warm water of the shower they were soon reinvigorated. Rather than going down on Mark, however, Paul turned him around and, sinking to his knees, started licking around the rim of his anus. Mark squirmed, turned on by the new sensation.

The towel was still damp, so they just brushed off the heaviest of the water on their bodies. Mark led Paul back into the bedroom and signalled for him to lie on the bed. Paul grasped his hard on and held it upright. On hands and knees Mark licked it up and down. He shuffled around until his arse was over Paul's face. When Mark passed the lube back Paul understood and lubricated a finger which he slowly pushed up Mark's arse.

Mark had played with butt plugs before. He had trained himself to relax his sphincter to take in ever larger objects. He stopped licking Paul's cock as two and then three fingers were thrust into him, so he could enjoy the sensations.

Grabbing the condoms, Mark unfoiled one and rolled it down Paul's hard on. Paul passed the lubricant to him and Mark smeared it all over the condom. Then he moved around so that his cock laid on Paul's chest as he reached back for the younger man's hard on.

With great care, and a little guidance from Paul, Mark brought the hard on to his arse. Certain it was lodged firmly, he relaxed and began sinking back onto it. The head pushed slowly past his sphincter, causing them both to cry out when it passed the barrier.

This was different to playing with a butt plug, Mark realised. There was a warm body under him, straining to thrust into him at its own pace. He sank farther down Paul's cock until it was as deep in him as it could go. Then he started moving up and down in short movements. Paul started thrusting and pulling out under him, matching his rhythm. Then he grasped Mark's hard on and let it slide through his hand as they moved.

They were both too excited for it to last as long this time. Under Paul's ministrations Mark soon came, splattering semen across his lover's hairless chest. He began rocking back and forth harder and faster, willing Paul to come in him. Their bodies slapped together and slid apart faster and faster until Paul thrust up and held his position as he came.

They sank slowly back to the bed. Mark moved slowly forward, until Paul popped out of him with a jerk that made him moan. Then he dropped sideways and stretched out on the bed. He drifted off for a while.

When Mark woke again Paul was stood at the end of the bed, towelling himself off. "Another shower." he said with a smile. "I, er, thought I should head home. I wasn't going to wake you. Thought I'd leave a note."

"No worries." Mark watched Paul dress. "We should do that again some time." he suggested when Paul was fully clothed.

"Maybe." Paul offered. "I'll let myself out. See you some time next week."

* * *

Mark was distracted for the whole of the next week. He kept thinking back to the sex over the weekend and getting excited. He didn't know if it would happen again. In fact, he didn't have any contact details for Paul, so he couldn't call him and ask. He just had to wait until they next met.

Which was on Friday evening, in the pub. Paul arrived halfway through Mark's first pint. As they were in company they simply nodded recognition and muttered hellos. Paul hung his jacket over the back of the chair next to Mark and headed to the bar.

Two pints later Paul announced, "I shouldn't have any more. At least not until I've eaten. Does anyone else want to go for a curry?"

Paul's knee was pressed against Mark's leg. He took this as a signal. "It's been a while since I've had a curry. Yeah, I'm in." Everyone else around the table shook their heads. Paul had judged the suggestion well.

They drank up and bade their farewells before heading for the bus stop. "Of course," Paul said, "I have some chicken korma at mine. We could go there."

"That sounds like a good idea."

So they caught a bus in the opposite direction to the one they'd claimed. Paul led the way to his flat. Even before they'd got through the door Mark had an erection so hard it was almost painful for it to be trapped in his trousers. Paul noticed, and before putting the key in the flat's door he reached down and gently squeezed it through the fabric.

As soon as they were through the door Paul slammed it shut and pushed Mark up against it. He dropped to his knees and quickly released Mark's hard on. "I've been thinking about this all week." He licked the whole length and took the head in his mouth and soon had his lips far down the shaft.

Mark squirmed against the door. "Me too." he managed.

Paul was moving his head back and forth rapidly and smoothly. He paused at the top of every few swoops along Mark's cock to swirl his tongue around the head. Mark knew he was going to come soon. "Don't..." he managed just before the semen started to pump into Paul's mouth. Paul managed to catch all of the sticky fluid on his tongue, before swallowing it with a little wince.

Mark slid down the door. Paul sat back against the wall opposite. "I want you to fuck me. On the sofa."

"Okay." Mark quickly stripped out of his clothes and let Paul lead him to the living room. On the end of the sofa was a bag with all the lube and condoms they could possibly need. Mark felt himself getting hard again. He sat and examined the contents of the bag, but his attention quickly returned to Paul as the younger man started to undress.

"I thought I should get some supplies of my own." Paul announced. "I even got myself another butt plug." The plug wasn't in the bag. When Paul turned and bent over to remove his trousers and boxers Mark spotted the flared base, wedged between taut buttocks.

"You had that in when you were in the pub?"

"Of course. It took a bit of time to get it in, that's why I was so late. And there was only so long I could keep still with it in there. That's the real reason I had to leave the pub. Do you want to pull it out?"

Mark was rock hard again. "Yes." he managed.

Paul moved back until his calves were against the cushions of the sofa, either side of Mark's legs. Mark reached up to grasp the base of the butt plug. He tugged at it gently, and Paul's buttocks tightened as he tried to hold it in. He sighed as Mark pulled harder and drew the plug further out, then cried out as it popped past his sphincter.

Mark lubed up two fingers and slid them into Paul's arse. Clumsily, with his other hand, he tried to open a condom. Eventually he had to use his teeth to tear the wrapper open, then carefully rolled it down his cock. Impatiently, he squirted lubricant onto it. "Okay." he announced, pulling his fingers out of Paul.

Carefully, supported by Mark, Paul sat back and sank down toward Mark's hard on. As he got closer Mark gave him finer guidance, until his cock lodged at the rim of Paul's anus. Now they moved more carefully. Paul slowly put his weight onto Mark's cock, easing down it until he sat with it fully inside him.

Mark reached around and grasped Paul's hard on, gently stroking it. Paul sighed and started moving, as best he could. He couldn't move up and down very easily, so he ground back and forth instead. This was a slower session than their previous times. Mark wasn't making big movements inside Paul, but was stroking his cock hard and fast. It wasn't long until Paul leaned back as he came. His arse squeezed hard on Mark's cock, making him call out in sympathy.

When Paul had relaxed again he lifted his feet onto the front edge of the sofa and braced his hands against the rear cushion. Very carefully he lifted himself up and let himself back down again. It still wasn't as long a thrust as Mark would have managed if he'd been on top of Paul, but it was more than they'd managed before.

Even with Mark supporting him, Paul couldn't keep on moving up and down for long. Mark eased him onto his side and began thrusting into him. He was soon moving harder and faster as he got closer to coming. Paul was hard again, he reached down and stroked his semen slicked cock as he urged Mark on.

Mark came with a grunt, holding himself deep in Paul as he filled the condom. He put his hand over Paul's and together they carried on stroking the hard on together until the younger man came again.

They lay on the messy sofa for a while, recovering. Paul wiped himself, and the cushions, down with his T-shirt. Neither of them was sure what they were supposed to do immediately after sex. An urge to cuddle was balanced by discomfort. Without words they went through to the bathroom and showered.

When they were cleaned and dressed Paul heated the curry he had prepared. Sat on the sofa eating the curry and watching television he finally asked, "What are we doing? Is this, I don't know, a relationship?"

"I'm not sure. I've never had a relationship with another man."

"Don't start on I have never, that's how we got here."

"Do you want to keep on fucking?"

"Yes."

"So let's fuck every so often. No commitments."

"Fuck buddies?"

"I guess so."

"I've never had a fuck buddy."

* * *

They didn't know what being fuck buddies entailed. Neither of them was about to search the internet for guidelines. So they made it up as they went along.

Occasionally one of them would text the other, asking if they were doing anything later. They didn't always get together, and more than once they ended up playing video games without having any sex. Nights out at the pub didn't always end with sex and a shower, either, but some of their hottest sessions lasted from Friday night to Saturday afternoon. Once they fucked and sucked all the way through to Sunday night. It didn't seem that anyone else noticed their relationship. They were quiet about it, often even leaving events at different times. Neither of them expected the relationship, such as it was, to go on for long. Something would come along to change things.

* * *

That something was Julie. She moved into the flat below Mark's. With nothing else to do on the Saturday she arrived, he offered to help shift her boxes. "Thanks. I had help packing, but told them I'd be okay at this end. Pride's a terrible thing." She was short and slim, with cropped black hair, a pretty round face and grey eyes. Mark might not have offered to help a less attractive new neighbour. "Here. Can you be careful with that, it's crockery."

Paul turned up halfway through unloading the van. He watched, bemused. "I was dropping by to suggest video games or the pub, but this looks productive." He started shifting boxes too.

In next to no time they were done. Boxes were arrayed around Julie's flat, directly under Mark's, arranged by the room their contents were for. Julie beamed as she closed the door. "Thanks so much for the help. I've got to get the van back and pick up my own car. But I'd like to buy you two a meal, to say thank you for your help. How about tomorrow?"

Mark nodded, "Cool."

"About three?" Paul suggested.

"It's a date." Julie practically skipped down the stairs.

"I'm all sweaty now." Paul said after the front door had slammed closed.

"Shower?" Mark suggested.

* * *

After they'd dried each other off, at least, enough to generate erections, they walked from the bathroom to the bedroom. Paul lay down on the bed, invitingly holding his cock as close to vertical as he could manage. Mark straddled Paul's shoulders, angling his hips to aim his own erection roughly at Paul's mouth, and took his lover's hard on between his lips.

Paul tried his best to angle Mark into his mouth, but it just wasn't working. He laid the warm penis against his cheek and ordered, "Roll over. This'll work better if we're on our sides."

Mark managed the move without releasing Paul's cock head then, under direction, he arched his back and moved around until Paul could swallow him properly. They lay together, each gently exciting the other. They moved their lips up and down each other's shafts, swirled their tongues around the heads and even gently nipped with their teeth. Eventually Mark could hold out no longer. He panted over Paul's erection as the younger man sped up his head bobbing, coaxing him over the edge.

Mark came in Paul's mouth. Paul swallowed as much as he could of the semen, then licked around Mark's shaft and deep red head to clean them. When he could move again, Mark dedicated himself to taking Paul as deep as he could and sucking, licking and teasing him to orgasm. Then he too swallowed all he could and licked his lover's dick clean.

Sated, they lay where they were for a while. "Were you thinking of your new neighbour too?" Paul asked eventually.

"Yeah."

"What do you think?"

"I doubt she's as dirty as us."

"Maybe we should ask."

"How on Earth do we do that?"

"Haven't a clue."

* * *

Julie knocked on Mark's door, as promised, at three o'clock the following afternoon. Paul answered. "Come on in. He's trying to clear the level."

They watched Mark shoot his way down a corridor, turn a corner and get caught by heavy gunfire. When he died he shrugged and turned off the console and television.

"Where would you like me to take you?" Julie asked. She was wearing a light summer dress which came to just above her knees. When the light through the window caught it just right the fabric let some of the beams through, giving tantalising hints of the body it concealed.

"How about our local," Mark suggested, "it's just at the end of the street."

They chatted about the move on the way down the street. Paul pointed out his flat as they passed it. Across the road at the end of their street was the pub. It was a large building, set back from the road, which appeared grander and older than most of the houses around it. It gave the impression of once having stood there by itself, surrounded by fields, not noticing the slow crawl of urbanisation toward it.

The Sunday lunch crowd was busy. There were a lot of young, and not so young, professionals, and a large number of children. They managed to find a table outside, quickly stepping in to claim it as a family left, and settled down with the menus. After they had placed their food order and got the first round of drinks in Julie leant forward, inviting Paul and Mark to huddle closer so they could hear her conspiratorial whisper. "I know this might be rude, but I wanted to ask." she went red, "But, are you two, well....." she went an even deeper red, embarrassed as much by her inability to ask the question as the question itself.

"Are we?" Mark prompted.

"Are you gay?"

"Nope."

"But we do occasionally fuck." Paul chipped in.

Julie couldn't flush any redder than she already was, but it didn't subside as fast as it might have. "Oh, right. You're bisexual?" Mark and Paul nodded. "So you like women too?" Julie realised the redundancy of the question, but wanted them to confirm the answer for her. They both smiled and nodded. She appeared ready to ask another question, then thought better of it and sat back to take a gulp from her pint and cool down a bit. "How did you get together?" she managed after a moment.

Paul and Mark recounted the game of I Have Never and its dirty consequences. They kept their voices low so diners at nearby tables couldn't hear the tale, and they stopped completely when food and further beer arrived.

The subject of sex didn't arise again until they were on the way back from the meal. Julie took Mark and Paul by the hand as they walked tipsily along the street. "So..." she started, "In your relationship, is one of you the top and one the bottom?"

"We swap." Mark announced.

"But Mark's top more often." Paul conceded. "We should have more to drink." he announced, "This is my place and I have lots of bottles which should be emptied."

Paul produced beer from his fridge as soon as they were through the door. They took the bottles and sat on the sofa in the living room, Julie wedged between the two men. "I'm quite drunk." she announced, "But not too drunk to know what I'm doing."

"That's good to know." Mark said with a smile.

They drank quietly for a while. Julie drained her beer faster than Mark or Paul. "You're not trying to get so drunk you don't know what you're doing are you?" Paul asked.

"No. Just a little Dutch courage." she put down the bottle and laid a hand on Mark and Paul's nearest knee. "I've moved from a small town, where everyone knows everyone else's business. I'm here because of my new job, but I want to take advantage of being out of the gossip loop. It's a chance to be dirty."

"How dirty?" asked Mark as Julie's hand moved up his and Paul's legs.

"I don't know, yet. But it's great that I've met you two. I would really like to see you two make love. I've never seen two guys...."

"That could be arranged." Paul said with a little intake of breath as Julie's hand reached his crotch and began feeling the shape of his hard on through the material. "Of course, it would be great if you could help us." he added. He and Mark put their beers aside and reached down to help Julie open their jeans. As two hard penises were presented to her she glanced back and forth between them before reaching out and taking one in each hand and gently tugged and stroked at them.

Paul and Mark each laid a hand on one of Julie's knees. With no urging from them her legs spread wide. The hands moved up her thighs, pushing the hem of the dress before them until they revealed the white thong she wore.

Julie looked down, reddening and breathing heavily as she watched Mark start to unbutton her dress from the top and Paul start from the bottom. She couldn't concentrate enough to move her hands on their cocks any more, but they didn't seem to mind. Paul leaned in to kiss her, then Mark gently moved her head so he could lock lips with her. The last button was released and the dress fell open. Everyone stopped to look at what was revealed.

Julie had small, firm breasts. She had dared not to wear a bra and now, as Mark and Paul pulled her dress open, they were revealed to their gaze. Her nipples, already taut and sensitive, hardened and grew some more. Mark and Paul each reached for the nearest breast and ran their fingers around it. Julie began pumping both their cocks again, urging them on.

Mark bent down and took a nipple in his mouth. Julie threw her head back and moaned. Paul kissed and licked at her exposed throat. Suddenly, almost unexpectedly, Julie came. She shook with the delicious spasms. Paul and Mark looked at each other over the shaking girl and shared a grin before she relinquished their hard ons to reach up and pull both of them into a three way kiss.

Julie sat up, and Mark and Paul eased the dress off her shoulders and down her arms. They stood and offered her a hand each. She swayed to her feet, still shivering with happy aftershocks of her orgasm. Wearing only her shoes and the triangle of her thong she cuddled up to them and, with an arm around each of their waists pulled them closer, until the tips of their cocks almost touched as they rubbed against her belly. She sighed as they both started playing with her breasts again.

"Would you like to see me suck Paul's cock?" asked Mark. Julie nodded vigorously, still at a loss for words.

They led Julie to the bedroom and laid her on the bed. She sat up on her elbows and watched as Mark removed her shoes and Paul undressed. When Paul was naked Mark pointed to a spot on the bed close to Julie's head. Paul smiled and clambered up the bed until he was kneeling in the spot, his cock arching up just above Julie's wide eyes and his balls swinging tantalisingly close to her mouth. She raised herself a little and took one of those balls gently between her lips. Paul held perfectly still, but for a light trembling, as Julie played with the wrinkled skin of his ball sack.

Mark stripped and clambered up the bed on all fours. He moved around until he could lick the head of Paul's cock and then slowly take it into his mouth. Julie released Paul's ball sack and sank back to watch the live sex show going on inches from her face. "Wow." she managed, "This is so hot."

Paul put out a hand to brace himself against the wall as Mark sucked down his shaft. As he drew his mouth back up the erection it glistened with his saliva. Julie couldn't resist and lifted her head and twisted it to nibble at the underside of Paul's cock with her lips. Mark started doing the same along the top of Paul's hard on and his lips met Julie's just under the head. They both slid off the warm flesh to steal a kiss before Mark went back to licking around the head and Julie played with the ball sack.

It wasn't long before Paul announced, "Gonna cum." Julie's tongue traced all the way along the underside of his erection until it fought and played with Mark's at the head.

Mark wanted to swallow the hot red head and have it all to himself, but he also wanted to share it with Julie. He'd put his lips around most of the head and slurp off it then let Julie do the same. Paul came just as Mark was passing the baton. The first spurt landed on Julie's cheek before she could clamp her lips over the head. She sucked up semen then let the head slip out of her mouth so Mark could get his share.

As Mark and Julie licked the head of Paul's cock clean he slid back and into a sitting position. By the time they were certain there was no more semen to lap up Mark was draped across Julie's nearly naked body. His cock head rubbed along the edge of her thong. Looking down they could all see the fabric of the skimpy triangle stained with Julie's juices. "I want you to fuck me." she told Mark. "I want you both to fuck me." she said to Paul, "When you're ready."

"With pleasure." Paul assured her. He opened the drawer of the bedside cabinet and pulled out a packet of condoms. Julie pushed Mark onto his back and handed a condom to him. As he opened the foil and rolled the sheath down his shaft she knelt before Paul and urged him to remove her thong. He slid the knickers down and smiled at what was revealed, "Shaved." he said, wistfully. He ran a finger around the edge of Julie's naked lips and she let out a little groan.

Mark stroked Julie's buttocks and reached under them to slide his hand through her legs and lay a finger between the slick lips of her pussy. The finger slid into her and then he pushed it gently into her warmth as she began moving on it. Paul, meanwhile, had found Julie's clitoris, rising proud from the sheath at the top of her lips. He teased around it. He couldn't easily move to get his mouth over Julie's clit, so he licked at her breasts and nipples.

Julie arched her back, and would have fallen over backwards if Mark hadn't reached up with his spare hand to support her. "I'm supposed...." Julie started to announce, "I'm supposed to be fucking Mark." She quickly added, "Don't stop." before either of her lovers could think to.

Mark slid a second finger into Julie's slippery pussy and that pushed her over into orgasm. She shivered and trembled and savoured every moment, letting Mark and Paul support her as she did so. As she started to come down again they began to ease her down to the bed. This roused her, "No," she demanded, "I want Mark's cock in me. Now."

Paul helped Julie pull off her knickers and move until she straddled Mark, then helped guide his lover's cock into her slick and ready pussy. As the large hard on filled her it nudged her into another orgasm and she fell forward onto Mark's chest. "I don't think I can move though." she admitted. Mark began moving under her, short but very effective strokes. She grasped his shoulders and gasped in time to his movements.

Paul, behind Julie as Mark thrust in and out of her pussy, had a fine view. He reached down to cup a small, firm and perfectly curved buttock in each hand and started moving them in time with Mark's thrusts. This elicited a squeal of delight from Julie, and another orgasm.

With Julie's buttocks spread, Paul could see the puckered entrance of her anus. Now wasn't the right time to try to plug it, but he was confident that Julie would want to try anal sex. The thought made his growing erection twitch up tauter. He moved closer to Julie's arse and laid the hard on between the cheeks. He looked down at Mark, who quickly got the idea and stopped thrusting.

Julie's head popped up, she looked confused. "Hey, what happened? I was about to come. Again." Paul grasped her about the waist, pushed his cock between her arse cheeks and started grinding against her. He moved her up and down Mark's cock and, true to her word, she came.

Julie seemed to be having non stop orgasms as Paul moved her and Mark began thrusting again to accentuate the rocking. She squealed with particular intensity as Mark laid his hands over Paul's, urging him to stop, and thrust up as far as he could to fill the condom inside her.

Paul rubbed his cock up and down Julies butt cleft a few more times, thinking it was after play. But she looked round and announced, "Your turn."

"You're sure?"

"Oh yes. Yes. I want more."

Mark passed up a condom. As Paul put it on Julie lifted herself off Mark's cock. She took her time about it, as if she didn't really want to let it go. She made a little "oh." noise when it finally popped out. She struggled and moved around until she was lying on her back on Mark's chest, offering her shaven lips to Paul. Mark reached around and played with her nipples.

Mark spread his legs, splaying Julie's which were laid on top of them. Paul eased forward and laid his hands on Mark's shoulders for support. Mark guided Paul's cock to its target.

With incredible ease Paul slid his entire length into Julie. He could feel the tremble of a building orgasm in her body. He could also feel Mark's resurgent erection, which hadn't subsided all that much, nudging against his balls and perineum. He pulled out and slid gently back in. The tremble in Julie intensified. She stared up at him. "Faster. Please." she pleaded.

Paul's pace increased. Mark held Julie in place as she started to writhe under Paul's movements. She came again, crying out with pure bliss and shaking all over. Paul paused, half in Julie, and enjoyed the vibrations on his cock.

As Julie's latest orgasm subsided her hands weakly reached up to stroke Paul's arms. "More." Paul grinned, happy to oblige. He reached down and pulled Julie's legs so they stuck straight up, resting on his chest with her feet either side of his head. This changed the angle of his cock in her. She loved this.

With only a couple of thrusts from Paul, Julie was coming almost continuously. Mark held her in place, keeping her from shaking out from under Paul. Then he had an idea. Reaching up, and with help from Paul, he hooked a hand behind each of Julie's knees and drew her legs further back until they almost pressed against her chest.

The position squeezed the inside of Julie's pussy tighter and Paul groaned his pleasure at the increased pressure. He sped up his thrusts, driving into Julie and rocking her on top of Mark. The three of them were reduced to grunts and sighs. Even Mark felt he was close to coming, just from the hot sex going on above him, though Paul's balls rubbing against his dick helped.

Paul stopped thrusting. He grasped Mark's arms and held himself in place as he came. Julie squealed with joy at the feeling of the condom filling inside her. Then she fainted away with the pleasure.

Paul pulled gently out of Julie and he and Mark eased her legs down. She slid off Mark and lay beside him, grinning and utterly relaxed. As Paul and Mark pulled the sheaths from their cocks Paul looked down and recognised Mark's state of arousal. "Need a little help with that?" Mark just nodded.

Paul licked the semen, and slightly bitter taste of the condom, from Mark's hard on, cleaning it. Julie cuddled up to Mark's shoulder, resting her head on it and watching Paul give him a blow job through half closed eyes.

Mark was very close to coming and Paul recognised this. He swirled his tongue around the head then closed his lips over it just as Mark came. Julie grasped the hair on Mark's chest lightly as she watched Paul suck up the semen. "Kiss me." she told Paul. As they shared the sticky liquid Paul had lapped up she came again.

Paul lay down on the other side of Julie, who was drifting off to sleep. Mark and he stroked her naked body, causing mini orgasms with almost every touch. "I am so glad I met you two." she managed to say breathlessly.

"So are we." Mark replied.

"There's still so much I want to try." Julie purred. "I've never given two guys a blow-job at the same time."

"That can be arranged." said Mark.

"I've never tried anal. I want to have one of you in my cunt and one in my arse. At the same time."

"That will be our pleasure." grinned Paul.

"I have never had sex with a woman."

"That one's going to be a little trickier."

Rain Starts Play

Neither John nor Karen had believed in Internet dating. They had both signed up out of curiosity and only a little optimism. They had each had a couple of dates which convinced them they were right before they had found each other. After passing a few messages back and forth they arranged a date, which had gone well, and led to a second. They had kissed at the end of the second date. Nothing too racy, but more than just a quick peck on the cheek. For their third date they had arranged a Saturday together, with a picnic in the park before going to a mini music festival which was on near Karen's apartment building.

The three day run of good weather broke early on Saturday morning and it started to rain. And showed no sign of stopping. Staring at it from his kitchen window as he cleared away the breakfast crockery John sighed. He texted Karen, 'Looks like picnic in the park is off. Would you like to do something else?'

The response, almost immediate, was, 'Come into town. We can have a beer and decide what to do then. I'm not letting shitty weather spoil my Saturday. See you at noon.'

Cheered up by the invitation, John calculated he had enough time for a shower and a shave before umming and aahing over just what he should wear.

By the time John got to the pub, the same one their previous dates had started at, the effort he'd put into choosing his outfit had been negated by the shower that caught him on the way from the bus stop. Karen, already at the bar, looked at him and tried not to smile. "It's raining again?"

"It started bucketing down about a minute ago. I think I saw Noah down a side street."

Karen bought John a pint and they walked to the back of the pub. They sat side by side on a big leather sofa with a view of the whole pub and plotted their next move. Karen had a long raincoat, draped over the arm of the sofa, but beneath it had worn the same summer dress she would have if they had gone on their picnic. It stopped just below her knees and, when she crossed her legs and let one idly swing as she thought, John had shapely calves to appreciate. "Everything I had planned for today was outside." he admitted, "Do you have any ideas what we could do?"

"Well I had an idea for later on which was indoors. We could bring it forward."

"Okay. What was your plan?"

"I thought we could go back to my place, it's just across the road, and have sex." Karen delivered the suggestion with a smile then quickly took a drink of her wine.

"That sounds better than anything I was going to come up with. By a long way."

"I hoped you'd like it. Let's finish our drinks then head over when the rain eases."

* * *

Karen's apartment was on the third floor. They took the lift, which felt far warmer at the end of the short trip. Karen led John a short way along the corridor and into her apartment.

They stood just inside the door, momentarily uncertain. Their bags dropped to the floor and they took a step closer. Karen stood on tiptoe and John leaned toward her and they kissed.

It started as a gentle, exploratory locking of lips and became wilder as their tongues played. John moved Karen back until she was against the wall then rested his hands on her hips. She reached up to hold his shoulders.

John's hands slid down Karen's dress until they traced over the skin of her thighs. He gently ran his fingers over the soft skin then started to move them back up, catching the hem of her dress on the way. They broke off the kiss and both looked down as he raised her dress to reveal her knickers. She looked at him and he raised a grin. Then he dropped to his knees.

John let Karen's dress fall over his head as he knelt before her. She giggled at the sight of it ballooning out in front of her, but the sound turned into a squeak as he started kissing her thighs. John's lips teased up her left leg from her knee to the edge of her knickers. She could feel his breath against the material and knew he could smell her excitement. He kissed her through the cotton then reached up with both hands to pull the knickers down.

Karen had black pubic hair trimmed back from lips which were darkening and filling out as John watched them. The lips pulled apart as he teased them, glistening. He savoured the smell, and felt the heat, of Karen's excitement. His tongue licked along the ridged lips from bottom to top and back again.

Karen shivered with the sensations spreading out from John's tongue. It had been too long. A little voice nagged at her, trying to spoil the moment. It reminded her that other men had gone down on her, but only long enough to show willing and never long enough to get the job done. She pushed the voice away as John's tongue delved into her and made her whimper.

Karen tried to spread her legs, to give John more access, but her knickers were around her ankles and wouldn't let her. John sensed the problem and blindly reached out to unhook her right foot from them. He lifted her right leg and hooked his shoulder under it, then did the same with her left. Karen let herself be supported by John and the wall, the precariousness of it just adding to the thrill.

John pressed the flat of his tongue against Karen's lips, then drew it up and moved it side to side. Karen was grasping her dress tight where it wrapped around John's head and she pulled him onto her even tighter. Her gasps and squeaks of pleasure became more drawn out until finally the feelings were so intense she couldn't find a sound which summed them up. John knew he'd found the sweet spot and he ground his tongue around it, flicking the tip against Karen's lips for added pleasure.

Karen's muscles were contracting and relaxing as climax drew closer. Her pumps hung off her toes, dancing with every little shiver of pleasure until, as she came, she kicked them off with a jolt.

Orgasm washed over Karen, violent shivers of joy followed by warm washes of ecstasy. The lights flashing behind her eyes flared and faded as the tension flowed out of her. She felt soft and limp and intensely happy. John ran his tongue along the edge of her puffed up and sensitive lips and warmth flowed through her again.

John gently helped Karen slide down the wall until she sat against it with her dress up to her waist and legs spread. He sat cross legged before her, stroking her feet and lower legs, sending tingles through her every time. They smiled at each other and she beckoned him closer. Karen lazily wrapped an arm around John's neck and drew him closer to kiss him. He tasted of her own juices, a little sweet, and she realised she liked her flavour. She licked around his mouth then gasped through another, smaller, orgasm just thinking about the naughtiness of it.

Their kisses grew hotter again. Karen drew back to ask, "Would you like to see my bedroom?"

John helped her to her feet. Her dress fell again and she almost looked decent. She kicked her knickers off her foot and led John to the bedroom.

The room was dominated by a king sized bed, the covers flung aside when Karen had got up in the morning. One wall was dominated by windows and a door out onto a balcony, another by floor to ceiling mirrored doors to the built in cupboards. There was a chair in the corner opposite the door, a bedside cabinet cluttered with a radio, light and several books and some clothes scattered around the floor. "Sorry for the mess. I couldn't decide what to wear this morning." She started to pick up the clothes, then thought better of it. "Take your clothes off." she told John.

As John sat on the bed to take off his shoes the little voice came back to nag Karen again. No guy had ever gone down on her so enthusiastically, obviously he was compensating for something. She didn't want to listen to the voice, but she prepared to be disappointed.

John pulled his T-shirt off and dropped it on top of his shoes and socks. He wasn't buff, there was the hint of love handles, and he had dark and unruly hair across his chest. His chinos followed the T-shirt. Karen found she was biting her lip, a little nervous flutter in her stomach. The bulge in the front of John's boxer shorts was promising. He spotted her expression, smiled, and stood and walked over to her.

John took Karen's hands and laid them on his boxer shorts. She hooked her fingers into the waistband and drew them around to the front. She pulled the waistband out with her left hand and reached in with her right, grinning at what she found. The little voice was wrong again. She hooked her fingers around his large, stiff hard on and moved them up and down the soft skin.

Unwilling to let go of her prize, Karen started pushing the boxer shorts down with her left hand. He helped her, then stepped out of them when they hit the floor. Karen cupped his balls, squeezing them gently and lifting them. She wanted to repay the pleasure he'd just given her. She also wanted him in her right now. She didn't want to let go of his lovely large cock. She was lost for what to do.

John reached around to unfasten Karen's dress, then pushed it off her shoulders until it fell and revealed her bra. Reluctantly, she released his manhood and let the dress drop to the floor. She turned so he could unclasp her bra. Now they were both naked they looked at each other in the mirror. "Fuck me." Karen told John's reflection.

Karen climbed onto the bed and threw the covers off it. She lay down with her head resting on the pillows. Spreading her legs she reached down to split her slippery, sensitive labia with her fingers. "There are condoms in the top drawer." she pointed at the bedside cabinet with her free hand. She watched as he ripped the foil wrapper and rolled the sheath down his hard on. "I thought they were going to go past their use by date." she announced dreamily as he clambered over to her.

They stared down between their bodies as John poised over Karen. The fingers of her right hand were slicked with her own lubricating juices where she had been playing with herself. She slid them up and down John's hard on then grasped it and pulled it down toward her pussy.

Karen felt so open, so ready to accept this hard warm cock. It slid in easily and slowly filled her up. She came again before John was even halfway into her, shivering up and down her body and pulling him down to kiss him hard.

John pulled out and thrust back in, deeper this time. Karen felt her next climax building. She lifted her legs around John's waist and clasped them behind his back just as delicious tingles ran through her again.

John watched the beautiful face below him, loving the expression of pure joy. She seemed to be coming non-stop, lost in pure pleasure. He could feel his own orgasm approaching. His balls had pulled up into his body and his shaft was throbbing. He lowered his head to kiss Karen. After a moment she realised what he was doing and kissed back, her hands clasping at his head to pull him closer. John gave one last, deep thrust as he came and held himself deep in Karen as he felt the semen pump out of him.

* * *

They lay together, kissing occasionally. Karen rested her head on John's chest and ran fingers through the soft hair on it. She liked the smell of him. He smelt manly, and of recent sex. She played with one of his nipples and was amused when it stiffened under her touch. With an ear against his chest she could hear his heartbeat speed up. She glanced down the length of his body.

John's penis was stretching and rising. She squeezed the nipple and the cock twitched. John's heart ran faster for a few beats. Karen reached down and ran a finger along the hard on's ridge all the way down to the balls. It had grown some more before she ran the finger back. She helped the foreskin pull back from the dark red head.

It would be a shame to waste such a big happy hard on. Karen rolled across to the bedside cabinet and pulled out a condom. John was up on his elbows and watching her. They shared a smile before she tore the foil open and rolled the sheath down the warm cock. She bit her lip as she stared down at the gently twitching penis then swung a leg over John's body.

John could feel the warmth from Karen's pussy as it hovered over his cock. He grasped the shaft and held it steady as she lowered herself. Warm, wet lips split around the head and her mouth formed a little O as it entered her. The O grew as the head passed the lips and the walls of her pussy clasped at it. Her thighs were quivering as she eased herself gently down the shaft. The cock filled her more and more until she was sat right down on it. Their pubic hair meshed and twisted together.

It felt like a victory, sitting on John's cock, commanding all his attention. She looked down at the pale skin of her thighs against the darker, hairy skin of John's torso and knew she wanted to see that contrast in as many positions as possible.

John craned up, angling for a kiss. Their tongues played over and around each other then Karen kissed around John's mouth. He lay back at her signal. Karen rested her hands on his shoulders and grasped them as she started moving on his cock. He reached up and played with her breasts.

They looked at each other's expressions, reading how much they were each enjoying the sensations. John thrust up at Karen as she slid down and she made little "Oh" sounds each time. Every few times she stopped and ground against the base of John's cock.

Karen sat up straight and looked down at John's cock where it was lodged in her. He reached a hand down and moved their pubic hair aside so they could both get a better view. The pink nub of her clitoris was revealed by their explorations, inviting attention. John clasped thumb and forefinger over the hood which didn't quite cover the bud, squeezed them gently together and began moving them up and down.

Karen let out a little squeal and shivered from her thighs outwards. John relaxed his grip, until she managed to command, "Don't stop."

As John's fingers moved in circles Karen couldn't help but grind against his cock in response. She moved her hips back and forward, savouring the sensations as John pressed against different parts of her vagina walls. She was going to come before he did, she was certain, but she couldn't make herself slow down.

Karen started moving up and down again, drawing out the building climax a little longer. John lost his grasp on her clitoris. He pressed the flat of his hand against it and let her movements drive the rubbing. Just a few moments of this sent her over the edge. Her legs clasped John tight as she held herself suspended over him. Her pussy clasped only the head of his cock, pulsing around it. Every time she felt her climax subsiding she sank a little on the shaft, lifting it again.

When she had taken all of John's cock back into her Karen laid on his chest. She purred as he clasped her buttocks and squeezed the cheeks then gently began moving under her. Little aftershock orgasms made her shiver and sigh. John paused for a moment and she stretched her legs along his, pressing them together to clasp his cock tighter. He appreciated this, responding with faster thrusts and holding her closer to keep from throwing her off.

Karen kissed John's neck and chin, holding on to his shoulders. John's thrusts lost their rhythm as he approached climax and he cried out as he came. He shivered under her and sank back. Karen lifted her head and moved up until she could kiss him on the lips.

They lay together for a while, until John rolled over and slid Karen off him. He pulled out of her and turned away long enough to tug the condom off and tie it. With it discarded he cuddled up to Karen and they kissed. After a while she sighed, "I'm hungry."

"Sex is hard work." Karen giggled at John's observation.

"Let's get some food." Karen sat up and stretched.

* * *

There was a pile of flyers from fast food restaurants beside the phone in the hallway. "I never really learnt to cook." Karen admitted. She had pulled on John's T-shirt, which reached halfway down her thighs, and he was in his boxer shorts. She held up a flyer from a Chinese restaurant for John's approval. When it got the nod she took it and the phone handset into the living room.

After they had made their decisions and placed their order Karen stood and pulled the T-shirt off. "I'm going to have a shower. They shouldn't be here before I'm done."

John dressed, just in case their food did turn up whilst Karen showered. He turned on the television and flicked through the channels, not really paying attention as he sat in a happy post coital haze.

Karen returned some minutes later, wearing shorts and a white T-shirt. John had been half way across the room to start checking out her DVD collection. He was sure he looked guilty, but she didn't seem to notice. "Your turn." she told him.

John's surfing had ended on one of the history channels. There was a programme about the Romans on. Karen didn't bother changing it or turning the television off. She pulled her feet up onto the sofa, hugged them to her and sat with her head on her knees, watching Centurions march.

The intercom rattled. Karen uncurled and pulled the handset off the wall. She buzzed the downstairs door open and was standing by the open front door when the delivery man got out of the lift. John was hurriedly patting himself down with a towel as Karen walked past the bathroom door with a bag full of food. "Don't bother getting dressed." she grinned.

John didn't feel as self conscious as he'd expected, standing naked outside the kitchen and watching Karen empty food onto plates. She smiled at him and handed him a plate and cutlery. There was a table before the picture window and, despite the curtains still being open, that was where they sat and ate. Karen ran a bare foot up and down John's legs. She couldn't see his rising erection, but her smile said she expected it.

They didn't talk much as they ate. Sex really was hungry work. When they were done Karen piled the plates up and walked around the table. She stood before John and signalled for him to turn his chair around. Smiling at his hard on she knelt before him.

Karen cradled John's balls and kissed them both. Then she licked up the shaft to the head, swirling her tongue around it. John clasped the seat of the chair and watched Karen's lips slide over the dark red head of his cock. She drew them back up until they were just kissing the tip, then lowered them again, swallowing more this time.

John pulled himself down onto the chair, trying to plant himself in place and not make any movements which might put Karen off her vital task. She could take just over half his length comfortably, and began moving her lips up and down it. As she sped up John hooked his feet around the legs of his chair to brace himself further.

Karen stopped her movements, her lips clasped tight around his cock and the coarseness of her tongue rubbing against its underside. John groaned as she pulled back up his hard on, making loud and theatrical slurping as she released the head. She grasped the shaft and started moving her hand up and down it, staring up at John and smiling as she did. She teased him, licking around the base of his cock and kissing his balls.

John's hard on twitched as his orgasm approached. Karen moved quickly to lock her lips over the head again just before he came. She sucked the semen up, swallowing the sticky liquid. To gasps from John she licked the come up, cleaning the head and shaft.

Karen rested her head on John's knee and watched as his erection subsided. A small drop of come formed at the slit of the still red head. Karen reached out a finger and gently lifted it off. She smiled to see the cock twitch and grow a little again as she licked the semen off her finger.

Karen sat back, a hand on each of John's knees. "Do you want to stay the night?" she asked.

"Yes." John replied, still in a happy daze from the blow-job

Karen stood and offered John her hand. She led him to the sofa, sat him down and curled up with her head on his lap. John ran a finger along the edge of her exposed ear and down around her neck. She purred and squeezed his thigh. She was tired, in a warm and happy way, but still horny. The warmth in her pussy told her what she wanted to do just as soon as she had her energy back, and John's gentle touch was sending tingles through her which kept that warmth stoked.

The television was still on, but the subject had moved on from the Romans to the Second World War. This was the sort of thing which, left to his own devices, John could happily watch for hours on end. But he felt it was best not to admit to that. He picked up the remote and offered it to Karen. She shook her head, "You choose."

As John flicked through the channels his hand absently stroked Karen's arm and side. She rolled onto her back and stretched out, there was just enough room on the sofa. She rested her hands on the top of her thighs, framing the target she wanted him to aim for. Her nipples had stiffened and tingled against the material of her T-shirt. John pinched the material just below her left breast and tugged it down, rubbing cotton against the hard point and raising a light sigh.

John was still moving through the channels with the controller in his right hand, but was concentrating more on what his left was doing. He tweaked Karen's nipples and cupped her breasts through the cotton of her T-shirt. She hooked her thumbs into the waistband of her shorts and tried to push them down. They'd only go so far, though, as the drawstring which held them up was pulled too tight. John spotted this and reached down to pull the bow out of the drawstring.

Karen pushed her shorts down just far enough to reveal the bush of her pubic hair. She stared up at John, who smiled down at her. Not taking his eyes from hers he moved his hand around her belly button, teasing, then down under the waistband. Karen's left hand slid into her shorts and rested itself on top of John's. He got the message and let her guide his fingers.

Their fingers, held together, slid through her pubic hair, then, pressed flat, began to move in a circle. John raised his eyebrows, asking if he was doing this right. Karen nodded, absolutely. She spread her legs and tried to push her shorts down with her free hand.

The circles around Karen's clitoris became narrower then turned into more of an up and down motion. She stopped at the bottom of one of these sweeps and pushed down with her forefinger, between the slick lips of her labia. She made John curl his finger into her then began the up and down movements, now with an added thrusting and greater urgency.

Karen was aware of something warm and smooth rubbing against her cheek. She shifted her focus and became aware of John's hard on rearing over her. She gave up trying to push her shorts down and stopped guiding John's hand so she could reach up and grasp the erection. She twisted so she could run her lips over the underside of the cock and occasionally kiss the head.

John pushed another finger into Karen. She started swaying her hips back and forth, helping the fingers move inside her. Her lips moved up and down the underside of John's cock whilst her right hand pulled the skin over the head.

The fingers inside her pussy felt good, but Karen wanted John's cock again. She'd slipped a condom into the tiny pocket of her shorts and now she fumbled it out, dropped it and grabbed it again. When she held it before John he got the message. She sighed as his fingers withdrew from her, but she grabbed his hand and held it so she could lick the taste of herself off them.

As John rolled the condom down his hard on Karen slid off the sofa. She pushed the shorts off and knelt in front of the seat. When he was ready he moved round behind her. His hands softly ran down the curves of her buttocks, then back up to the small of her back- where Karen discovered she had another erogenous zone and let out a sigh.

John's hands grasped a cheek each and gently spread them, revealing her arsehole. She felt exposed and excited. She almost wanted him to try to push his cock in, even though she knew it would need lube and patience to do it properly. Maybe one day soon, for now his aim was lower. The hard head of his knob slid along her pussy lips then gently eased in, she was excited enough to make it a hands free job.

Grasping her around the waist, John pushed slowly into Karen. He held himself as deeply inside her as he could for a moment, until she was certain she could feel the pulse in his hard on, then began just as slowly pulling out. She didn't want to lose the feeling of being filled and she pushed back as he moved. It was like a series of mini thrusts as he moved a little out of her and she pushed back to reclaim his cock.

When John was as far back as he wanted to go, his hands around Karen's waist suggested she move forward. She moved until only the head of his hard on was in her, then pushed back again, reclaiming it all. Her next move wasn't as far, but she came back faster, and soon she was rocking back and forth along John's cock. She drew a gasping breath just before every thrust back and let out a panting victorious cry when she had the whole of him in her again.

Karen lost her rhythm as she grew more excited. Eventually she had to stop moving and lay her head on her arms on the soft cushions of the sofa. John took up the thrusting, his thighs slapping against hers every time he was deep in her. Karen raised her head to let out little cries of encouragement then a shout of joy as they both came together.

They spooned on the floor for a while until Karen stood and led John to the bedroom.

* * *

It was still raining on Sunday morning. Karen heard the patter of drops hitting her window as she roused from a deep and pleasant sleep. She'd been having very dirty dreams and woken horny. Luckily there was someone in the bed who could help her with that.

John wasn't quite awake when he felt fingers lightly playing with his hard on. He stretched and sighed at the sensation, then eagerly responded to Karen's kiss. Together they threw the duvet aside. Karen kissed her way down John's body and then up and down his cock before leaning over to get a condom from the bedside drawers. She rolled the sheath over the hard on and they both smiled at it.

Karen was still wearing the top from the night before, but nothing else. John ran fingers up the inside of her leg and round the outside of her pussy then gently rubbed one back and forth between them until it slid inside. Karen rotated her hips and let the finger move around inside her, smiling all the while. She threw her head back and smiled, then shivered as a light orgasm pulsed through her. She had been more horny than she'd thought, to come so quickly.

Clasping her thighs Karen held John's finger in her pussy for a while, then cast a glance down at his cock and nodded at it. He smiled and urged her toward it with a little move of his head. She released his hand and he helped her move over him. John held the base of his cock so it stood straight up and

Karen raised herself until she was level with the head, She shuffled forward and John ran the tip along her lips just like he'd run his finger. Slick with Karen's excitement, they split to let him in.

Karen lowered herself just enough to hold the head of John's cock between her pussy lips, keeping it there until her thighs began to tremble then sliding down it quickly. Impaled on John's hard on she grabbed the hem of her top and pulled it of. John's hands cupped her small firm breasts and fingers flicked over her stiff nipples. He began flexing his thighs and hips and making short thrusts into her. Karen took up the rhythm and soon they were moving together in rhythm.

Their movements sped up. Karen pushed both hands against John's chest to help her keep herself steady. John pinched her nipples between thumb and forefinger of each hand and their movements got faster still. Their thrusts were short, quick and so energetic the bed was beginning to move. Just as she thought she was going to lose the rhythm Karen felt waves of warmth and pleasure course through her body.

She collapsed onto John's chest, hugging him tight and kissing around his mouth. John's hands went to clasp her buttocks and he kept moving in her. Just as the tingling wash of pleasure from one orgasm was receding another broke over Karen. She bit John's shoulder and he held her tight as he came.

Only when the last shivers of after pleasure had drifted away did Karen slide off John's chest. "Morning." she said, her first word of the day.

✳ ✳ ✳

They slept some more, and eventually had breakfast at lunchtime. Sat at the table eating cereal they looked out of the window at a wet city which was beginning to sparkle in the sun. "You should go home before it starts to rain again." Karen suggested.

"I guess so." John knew he had to leave sooner or later, but he didn't like to admit it.

"Maybe next weekend we can have that picnic."

"Maybe."

"And maybe on Tuesday night you can come over and we can not have a picnic. Just like we didn't yesterday."

"Tuesday night?"

"I'm busy tomorrow."

"It's a date."

Fingers and thumbs

He lies on his back, eyes barely open, watching shadows and reflections from the traffic outside as they cross the ceiling. She has her head on his right shoulder, her slim arm draped across his chest. The fingers of his right hand gently stroke the sensitive spot at the base of her spine, just above her firm, smooth buttocks. Soft breaths ruffle the hair on his chest and her hand gently scrapes against a nipple.

Shifting slightly, he runs his left forefinger gently up her arm to her shoulder and back again, listening for the slight falter in her breathing as the sensations register. She's still mostly asleep, but still she responds by pressing her naked body against his. He runs his finger back along her arm, teasing each of her fingers when he reaches them.

This little hand is very talented. She draws with it, birds and animals and those special secret pictures of his naked body and hard, excited penis. Then she would make him lie back whilst she used those talented fingers to tease him. She'd start by running them gently over his skin, barely touching it, just as he was now with her arm. As he started to squirm, hands clasped behind his head to keep from reaching out, she'd start playing with his balls. Cupping them and holding them, she'd watch as the skin around them tightened and pulled them in toward his body. Then she'd grasp his cock, squeeze it, stroke it and play with it, building him up to orgasm. Sometimes she would dip her head to lick along the veins or swallow his hard on, but often she would finish him with a skilful hand job.

He turns her arm over and runs a finger around her palm. Now she's only pretending to be asleep, and all but grinding against his hips, her breaths shorter. Her hand clasps, but not tight enough to hold his finger as it moved to the sensitive skin on the inside of her wrist. She loved this light scratching just above her pulse. Her arm tenses as she pulls herself in closer. He traces down her arm to the inside of her elbow, another erogenous spot

With his right hand he presses into the small of her back, urging the movements of her pelvis as she pushes against him. He lifts her hand so her arm is standing straight up and she holds it there as he strokes up and down it.

Her fingernails are trimmed short. She had done it the week before for a very special treat. She had made him lie on his stomach, trapping his hard on against the bed. Then she had clambered up behind him and held his butt cheeks apart. She had lubed up her fingers and pushed one and then two of them up his arse, probing and then massaging his prostate. It had been so hot and so unexpected that he had come hard from grinding against the sheets. Next time, she had promised, she was going to fist him.

He brings her wrist down to his mouth, kissing the soft sensitive spot. She shivers and, as he kisses down her arm to her elbow, sighs out a little orgasm, the type she always loves to wake up to. He carries on stroking her arm as she subsides.

She moves, shuffling until she lies on her back too. Her right hand closes over his and she moves it up to close over a small firm breast. As he massages the breast and then runs fingers around the nipple her hand moves to her other breast. Almost in unison they pinch a nipple between finger and thumb, making her breath hiss in.

Now she moves again, reaching down for his cock and gently stroking it. He reaches down her back and cups a firm rounded buttock, then around it to the crinkly slick lips of her pussy. More shuffling and he can slide fingers into her, first one and then two. She likes that, and squirms against his hand, clasping his cock harder and giving it encouraging strokes.

Turned right around now, she teases with her mouth right by the head of his hard on as her hand moves up and down it faster. He pauses just long enough to push a third finger into her. She loves that and pushes back at them. This isn't the slow subtle hand play they sometimes indulge in, but a fast and sweaty fuck. He thrusts his fingers in and out hard and she cries out in pleasure.

Her hand is moving faster and harder up and down his cock and his hips are thrusting up at her. She kisses the head of his cock each time it's close enough. She closes her lips over the head just as he comes, swallowing the semen as it spurts out. A shiver runs through her body as she too comes.

With his fingers still in her he can feel her pussy twitch with happy little aftershocks. She curls up beside him, squeaking as he finally pulls his fingers out, lightly playing with his still half hard cock. Maybe they'll get up now, or maybe he'll get hard again and she'll straddle him and ride him until they come again. It's always the best way to wake up.

Tied

She is helpless.

Her hands are tied together at the wrists and held over her head, fastened to the bed so she can hardly move them. Her eyes are covered so she can't see anything at all, the velvet sleep mask soft against her face. Naked and vulnerable, her other senses are working overtime. The freshly laundered sheets feel soft against her sensitive skin. She can hear the creak of the floor as his weight moves on it. Even with the room as warm as possible a shiver still runs runs through her.

She concentrates on the sounds, hoping they will tell her where he is. Unconsciously her legs start to spread apart. When she realises she's doing this she wills them back together again, but they don't want to move. Traitorous limbs, she thinks, a tremble starting in them. She hasn't heard him move yet and already her heart is beating faster and she feels herself getting wet with anticipation.

There's the sound of the floorboard creaking again, then the rustle of a T-shirt hitting the floor and the clinking of a belt buckle opening. He's going to join her.

Every last sound as he undresses excites her- belt being pulled loose, jeans dropping to the floor, shoes being thrown aside. Then it goes quiet again. Waiting for him to move she tests the bonds at her wrists. The towelling belt from his bathrobe is soft and stretchy, tied tight, but not tight enough to be painful. If she wants, she can struggle free. Not that she wants to.

He's on the bed. Maybe just leaning on it, but the mattress deforms around his weight and she feels herself tilt toward him. She tries not to make it obvious how much she needs him to touch her, though she knows her hard nipples are giving her away. Her heart's beating so hard she wouldn't be surprised if her breasts weren't vibrating in time.

There'll be a smile on his face, she's sure. He always has a happy and appreciative expression when he looks at her naked. Now it's probably more of a mischievous grin as he considers everything he can do with her at his mercy. Before she can help it she's straining toward him, arching her body toward where she's sure he is. He kisses her.

It's just a light brush on her lips, but it's first contact. She lets her body melt back down to the bed. He will come to her, even if he'll drive her crazy doing it, she can stop trying to find him. He kisses her again, this time on her cheek. Light pecks tickle her left shoulder then all the way up her arm.

The weight moves off the bed. She pulls at the restraints, trying to follow him, making a plaintive squeak, but he's out of reach. It goes quiet, and that's making her hot in its own way. She's imagining all the things he might do next, and every one of them turns her on. Unable to stop herself, she's squirming against the sheets.

The pause draws out. She imagines she can feel the air moving against her skin, raising tingles and goosebumps. She raises her knees, drawing her feet up the bed and spreading her legs, trying to tell him where to go. It works, as she feels the foot of the bed bend under his weight and a thumb and forefinger gently grasping each ankle. Light kisses warm the inside of her knees and send twitches along her thighs. She's hot and wet and desperately wanting him to work his way down to her pussy. So, of course, he doesn't.

She's breathing hard and shivering all over with an orgasm that just won't quite peak. He puts his hands on her knees and gently moves them further apart. The slick, engorged lips of her pussy open to him, inviting him in. He must have a raging hard on, she knows he must. Surely he wants to put it in.

His fingers trace down the inside of her thighs. They skirt her mons and the edges of her sensitive lips. Then he runs a finger over her pubic hair and she's sure she can feel every strand as it's tugged. She wants him to slide just the one finger in, though she's sure he won't. The fingers move up to her belly button and take turns sliding around it. Her belly twitches and shivers as he touches her. His left hand presses into the bed beside her as he leans further forward and his right hand plays with one then the other of her breasts. He kisses around her right nipple, then takes it into his mouth, tongue flicking the stiff, sensitive tip.

Now both his hands are supporting his weight and he's kissing his way around her collar. She throws her head back so he can lick and nibble his way along her throat. A low, satisfied moan escapes her lips as he kisses her chin. Their lips meet and their tongues play against each other.

He pulls his mouth away, leaving hers open and panting. He hangs over her, so near but not quite touching her anywhere. If she closes her legs she can trap him, hold him to her. But she can't make them move.

He shifts his weight ever so slightly, she can feel him move. Then she can sense the hard hot head of his cock just outside her pussy. It shifts forward oh so slowly, gently pushing into her. She's so wet, so ready, so open, and he's so hard, that it slides in so so smoothly. She's holding herself down as the orgasm starts to wash over her. She feels it filling her, savours the victory, and, when the head is fully inside her, she lets out a cry of victory and pure pure pleasure.

Now she manages to hook her legs behind his, fooling herself that she's controlling his slow entry deeper into her. She's coming constantly, squeezing his hard on with every spasm, and feeling it intimately as it pushes into her.

He's completely in her, filling her, holding her. A hand reaches up and tugs at the end of the cord which holds her hands. The air is cool on her wrists. She holds them above her head for a while, then reaches up to pull him closer. She still has the mask on, but she doesn't need to see him when he's holding her so tight. He pulls out and back in, only a little, and sends shivers through her with every movement. They kiss, and he lifts the mask from her eyes. She blinks in the light and looks up at his face. He has that smile, so proud he's made her come so much and so happy to be making love with her.

With her legs pressed against the backs of his thighs and her hands on his waist she urges him to start moving in her. Each move, each stroke of his cock in her, raises aftershocks of pleasure in her. She changes the angle of her hips so his thrusts push against different parts of her pussy. As his movements become faster she plants her feet on the sheet and pushes up to meet him each time. She's lost count of the number of new peaks he's lifted her to. Now she wants him to come to.

He's moving faster, holding her butt cheeks in his hands and helping her lift off the bed. He's about to come, he has that far away look. One last thrust and he holds himself deep in her, coming hard. The warmth that fills her pushes her to another trembling sighing orgasm.

They sink together, slowly, to the sheets, rolling to lie side by side and kiss and caress and, later, sleep.

If you go down to the woods

"Let's go to my wood." Sally announced.

Mark looked out of the window and down the slope of the garden to the trees at its bottom. "Your wood?" Now he noticed the fence was broken by a stile.

"It came with the house. Mum and Dad planted a load of conifers along the motorway side when they first moved in, some of them are like twenty feet tall now. There are apple trees and a few old oaks. Come on, I'll show you around."

They walked down the garden from the bungalow. "The river runs around a couple of sides, and there's a fence. With the motorway it's completely enclosed and private." As Sally climbed over the stile Mark couldn't help but glance up the wide legs of her culottes, just catching a glance of her knickers. Sally stood on the other side of the stile, smiling back, "I used to come down here and take my clothes off and run around naked. I was only caught a couple of times."

"Really? How old were you when you did this?"

"The last time was last summer. I think it's time to do it again. Catch me." Sally ran off into the wood, disappearing behind a tree.

Mark was over the stile in a bound. When he rounded the tree Sally was nowhere to be seen, but her culottes had been dropped on the ground. There was a rustle, and Mark caught sight of Sally's black and white striped top and long legs as she skipped between smaller trees. She knew her way through the trees- it was her wood after all- he had to bumble through hoping not to trip over a root. He cut across toward the area she had been heading for.

Up ahead a fallen trunk leant against a much larger oak. Mark jumped up and grabbed one of the oak's branches, swinging over the deadwood. He tripped when he landed, tumbled and came to a halt staring at Sally's knickers, which hung from a branch. She was across a small clearing, smiling at him around a tree. With a giggle she disappeared from view.

Mark reached the tree in a few long, fast strides, but Sally wasn't behind it any more. A path, marked mostly by the grass being shorter, arced off from the tree and rounded a mini copse of hazel. Mark spotted movement in the gaps between the thin switches of wood. He trotted along the path to find it lead to another, larger clearing. Sally was in the middle of the open space, sat on a wooden picnic table.

She still had her striped top on, and her socks and shoes. When she stood up her exposed skin appeared far paler than normal against the dark greens and browns of the wood. The black triangle of her pubic hair stood out. "They've replaced the picnic table." she announced, "The old one was rotten through, though."

Mark advanced on Sally. "Is this one good and sturdy?" he asked with a grin.

"Well we didn't put it together, so maybe it can handle a little action." They had wrecked a small table when they had moved in together and been wary of furniture sex ever since. Sally reached down for Mark's belt when he was close enough. As she pulled it loose he pushed her back against the edge of the table. They kissed.

Sally fumbled with Mark's shorts. When she'd released the belt and unbuttoned them they dropped to his knees and then, after a shake of his legs, to the ground. She grabbed the waistband of his boxers and tried to tug them down, but they were hooked by the large hard on inside them. Sally tugged the elastic out and pushed it down. She ran the fingers of both hands up and down Mark's warm, stiff cock and giggled, "I found wood."

"Very funny." Mark just managed to keep a straight face. He helped her up onto the table and she reached down and helped guide his hard on into her.

Mark leaned Sally back as the head of his penis pushed at her pussy lips. With her guiding his aim he eased into her and they both let out a happy sigh. She lay back on the table and he lifted her legs, clasping them against his chest with his left arm whilst his right hand reached down to play with her breasts through the material of her top.

Her nipples were tight and hard and he could play with them through her top and bra. As he started thrusting gently in and out she began pulling her top up. Together they pushed the black and white stripes over the rise of her breasts, which were flushed with excitement. Mark eased the cup of the bra from her left breast and pinched the stiff nipple that popped out. She squeaked with joy and held his hand to her with both of hers.

Mark eased almost completely out of Sally then pushed slowly but forcefully back into her. She lifted her hips to help him deeper in. His thrusts sped up. He freed his hand from Sally's grip and grasped both her ankles, pushing her legs up and against her chest. She helped him by wrapping her arms around her knees and clasping her legs to her.

Mark gripped Sally's thighs tight and thrust hard and fast into her. Their breathing was short and sharp as they headed toward climax. Sally shivered as her orgasm built. She couldn't hold her legs back any longer. She let them go, Mark held them in place, and she clasped the edges of the table to keep herself from flying away.

Mark pulled Sally's legs back against his chest as the tempo of his thrusts changed again. He could see that she was close to orgasm, her eyes closed, head to one side, mouth wide open to let out little sounds of joy. Her legs tensed against his chest and the little sounds became a cry. Her back arched, her body shook and he could feel her pulsing around him. He gave a few more thrusts and couldn't hold back, coming deep inside her with a victorious shout.

They stayed like that for a while, gently coming down, until Mark eased his still half hard cock out of Sally. She let out a sad sound as it popped out of her. Mark let her legs slide easily down his arms until her feet lightly touched the ground. He stepped back and stripped out of his clothes.

"I've always wanted to do that." Sally sighed. She looked up but couldn't see Mark. Confused, she pushed up onto her elbows. But she didn't need to search far. Before she saw where Mark was she felt his hands running up the inside of her legs. She watched the top of his head as he kissed the inside of her thighs and worked his way to her warm tender pussy lips and reddened with the thrill and a little embarrassment.

Sally's crinkled lower lips were red and engorged and slick with their combined juices. Mark licked along them, tasting the combined tang of her pussy and the saltiness of his semen. Sally got self conscious whenever he licked his cum out of her, but she never made him stop and she always came hard. He ran the tip of his tongue the length of the lips and she shuddered with pleasure.

Sally draped her left arm over her flushed face, but reached down with her right to grasp Mark's hair and guide him. His tongue pushed deep into her, lapping up their juices. He moved further up and the flat of his tongue pressed against her mons and squeezed her clitoris. She loved that, panting with pleasure and urging him to press harder there.

With her legs crossed behind Mark's back, Sally let his head go and savoured his movements. She voiced her ecstasy loudly, far louder than she ever would indoors. Mark's right hand reached up and squeezed one then the other breast in time to his lapping. She found the hand, laced her fingers with his and clasped it tight as her orgasm mounted.

Any wildlife nearby would have scattered at Sally's scream as she came. She was always vocal, but this was astounding. She came down, catching her breath in little sobs, and realised she had Mark's head clasped tight between her thighs. She released him and he kissed his way back down her legs. When he stood she grabbed his hands and pulled him to her to kiss all around his face. "Thank you, thank you, thank you." she punctuated every kiss breathlessly.

Something warm and hard tapped against Sally's thighs as she kissed Mark. She broke off to look down and emit a low "Ooooh." of desire. Going down on her got Mark really, really hard, and even bigger than normal. The deep red bulbous head of his cock was just begging to be put in her, and she wasn't about to deny it. She could just lie back on the table and let him do her in the same position again, that had been glorious, but she wanted to try something else. She remembered another favourite part of this clearing and glanced across to check it was still there.

Sally stood and helped Mark pull her top and bra off. Now neither of them wore anything more than their shoes and socks. They stood in the sun for a moment, kissing in its warmth, before Sally stroked Mark's cock and led him across the clearing.

Two hemp ropes hung down from a large branch of the oldest oak in the wood and were tied to a thick plank which was just above knee height from the ground. Sally turned Mark and indicated he should sit on the swing. When he was settled on the smooth wood of the seat she took one of the ropes in each hand and moved to straddle him. Mark had other ideas. He looked up at the glory of Sally's slim body then kissed her belly. Two fingers sneakily and easily slid into her, stopping her in her tracks.

Sally grasped the ropes tight as Mark's fingers slowly moved in and out of her. She couldn't resist this interruption of her plans. Only as the shivers of orgasm started building in her did she look down and say, just loud enough to be heard, "I want you in me."

Mark gently pulled his fingers out and helped Sally. Carefully, and a little unsteadily, she threaded one leg between the rope and Mark's body. Then, with Mark supporting her, she did the same on the other side. Slowly she lowered herself onto Mark's cock. The big head pressed against her pussy lips, which opened slowly to accommodate it, then popped in slickly. Sally let out a victorious cry, which became an orgasmic moan as she slid further down the thick shaft.

Pressed tightly against Mark, and with him deep inside her, Sally let the orgasm rock through her. Lost in intense pleasure, Sally hardly noticed as the swing started to move. She hardly registered her feet rocking, and occasionally scraping, on the ground, even as she could feel his hair and skin move against her chest- particularly her so, so sensitive nipples. And she clasped at his cock as it made short but deep thrusts inside her. She was coming almost non-stop now, each time she ground against Mark she'd climb another mini peak on the plateau of constant orgasm.

Sally opened her eyes and the world swayed back and forth before her. She was dizzy and high and ecstatic and she clung tight to Mark. She didn't want this moment to end, but she was being worn out by joy. At her quiet urging Mark slowed, and eventually stopped, the swinging. They clung to each other and she still kept peaking just from his proximity.

Mark laid Sally gently on the grass. She made a sad sound when he pulled out of her, which became a squeak as the sensation brought on another orgasm. They lay side by side, enjoying the warmth of the day and listening to the wind in the branches. A patch of sunlight advanced across the clearing as they rested, until it shone fully on them and warmed them even more.

Sally looked down at Mark's cock, still big and stiff. "You didn't come again?" she said.

"No, but that's okay."

"Hardly. Before we leave this glade, you must come once more." She ran fingers over his chest. "In my mouth." she added lazily.

Sally kissed her way down Mark's chest to his twitching penis which was, it didn't seem possible, rising and getting larger again. She kissed the dark red head, kissed all the way down the underside to the balls- tasting herself on him- then licked back up. Shivers of joy were starting in her thighs and tummy just from doing this. If he touched her, stroked her in the right place, she'd be coming again.

Mark stroked the outside of Sally's thigh and she let out a moan of pleasure as she took his cock into her mouth. She moved around, away from him, to be between his legs as she sucked him. He'd given her such intense joy that now she wanted to concentrate completely on him. She held his hard on with one hand and his balls with the other as she moved her lips further down his shaft. When she had taken as much as she could she pulled back up slowly and licked around the head.

Mark stared straight up into the blue sky and grasped grass as Sally's mouth worked on him. She gave such great head, and he always came quickly when she did. She was concentrating on the fat, sensitive head of his cock, rubbing her lips over it as she moved it in and out of her mouth. He could feel he was about to come, and she could read the signals his body gave off. Her lips were clasped tightly to his cock so that when the semen started spurting out she didn't miss a drop. He shouted out as he came in her mouth.

They lay together in the sun until the beam passed away from them, then they dressed and left their forest pleasure garden, certain they'd be back for to enjoy it again soon.

One Dirty Night In Paris

Paris in July was glorious if a little hot. Mark was trying to fit in and be at least a little fashionable. His chinos were still freshly pressed- he was only a few days into his journey around Europe after all- with a light white ecru shirt and linen jacket. Only the hiking boots spoilt the ensemble. He was never going to be chic or even vaguely fashionable, but he could dress up better when in a city of style.

It was a seedy day, Mark had headed to the north of the city to photograph the Moulin Rouge then wandered along the road to the museum of erotica. He had resisted the invitations into the strip clubs, but had stepped into an adult emporium to check out sex toys and DVDs.

The longest wall of the shop was decorated with sex toys which varied in colour from realistic to ludicrous and in size from enticing to frightening. He had a sudden inkling for a butt plug to play with in his hotel room.

The choice was large, but after a few minutes pondering, Mark had decided on a two pack- one small, one large- which gave him something to start with and to work up to.

Mark's hand went for the butt plugs in blue, grabbing the box just as the woman beside him did. They both released the plugs and the pack dropped to the floor. As they both ducked to pick up the box their heads clunked together. As they stepped back from the pain Mark offered, "Pardon."

"Sorry mate." the woman replied, rubbing her head. The Aussie accent was a surprise.

"No worries." Mark didn't mimic her accent, but the phrase seemed appropriate. She was an inch or so shorter than him, with dark blonde hair tied back, sky blue eyes and a pretty oval face. She sported a light tan and was dressed more touristy, in sneakers, calf length jeans and a tight white T-shirt. He stared at her lovely round breasts straining against the cotton of her top then managed to drag his eyes back to her face.

"That's okay." The woman was obviously appraising Mark just as he had checked her out. It seemed she liked what she saw.

The initial eyeing up over with they both shuffled and slowly let their gazes drop to the sex toy in its box on the floor. "After you." Mark offered.

The woman picked up the butt plugs, but didn't put the box back on the shelf. She looked at the packaging, at Mark and then back at the box. "You were gonna buy these?"

"I was thinking about it." They had crowded closer together as they talked, a little embarrassed to be overheard.

"Have you ever used one before?"

"A few times. I've got some at home. But I'm here now and really wanted some."

"Is it hard to use them?"

"It takes a bit of relaxation, but it's worth it."

"For a fella. I know they work on your prostate. What about me?"

"I know a few women who swear by anal. They're fun to know."

"You got any advice?"

"Loads." The woman stared at the butt plugs for a while. "My hotel's only a couple of stops along the Metro and there's a good little café across the way from it. We could talk about it all there."

"Okay."

"I'm Mark, by the way."

"Kary. I'll get these. There anything else I need?"

* * *

They sat at the table, drinking espresso and then cognac, with the bag of sex toys- supplemented with lube and condoms, between them. In low tones they discussed the technicalities of anal sex. Mostly Mark told Kary about his experience of it, how he built up to it and what he enjoyed about it, but she threw in some tales of past boyfriends who had tried, and failed, to bugger her.

The more they talked about it, the more obvious it was they both wanted to, at least, try out the butt plugs. Hyper on caffeine and dizzy from brandy, Mark finally asked, "Shall we take this stuff to my room?"

"Hell yes."

Kary clasped the bag of sex toys and lube to her fine chest whilst Mark counted out Euro notes to settle the bill. Then they staggered across the road to his hotel.

The hotel was an old building on a corner, narrow and four storeys tall. The foyer was done out in dark wood panelling framing pale blue plaster adorned with early 20th century photographs of the city. When Mark collected his key the receptionist's gaze travelled to Kary and she gave a knowing smile. Who knew how many times she had seen this scene played out.

Mark's room was a twin on the second floor. He had chosen the single bed nearest the window to sleep in and unpacked his back pack onto the one nearest the bathroom. Kary dropped the bag on top of Mark's clothes. She looked around for a while, then came to a decision. Pulling a few items from the bag- Mark didn't see what- she announced, "I'm grabbing a shower and..... doing some stuff. I'll be a little while."

"Okay."

As the bathroom door closed Mark sat on the bed and pulled his boots and socks off. He adjusted the hard on in his trousers but didn't get undressed. He couldn't be sure what would happen next. He listened to the shower for a while, imagining the naked woman under the running water. This got him even more excited and his erection was almost painful trapped inside his trousers. He stretched across to lift the bag off the other bed and started going through it.

Kary had taken one of the tubes of lube and a syringe device for squirting it into her back passage. The sounds of the shower had stopped. Mark let his imagination run wild over what she must be doing now. She'd left the butt plugs, another tube of lube, condoms and other bits and pieces. Mark ripped open the box and took them out to compare them. The large plug was fatter and shorter than his own cock, he estimated. He was about to unzip his trousers and do a side by side comparison when Kary came back from the bathroom.

She wore only a pair of white knickers, which were a little damp and almost see through. Her breasts were just as good as her tight top had promised. They were round and firm, with a triangle of paler skin framing her nipples where she had recently been wearing a very skimpy bikini. The tan lines on her thighs suggested cut offs, rather than a thong, had made up the lower half of her outfit. Kary pointed at the plug Mark held. "So, er, how d'I get that thing... in me?"

"With great care and a lot of lube. But I think you should start with the smaller one."

"Okay. I used that syringe thing. I've already got a lot of lube up... there.

"Excellent. The next step is to take off your knickers."

Kary crossed her arms in front of her chest. "Nope."

"Nope?"

"Not until you even things up and take your clothes off too."

"Oh, well, if you insist." Mark stood and pulled the shirt over his head. He wasn't buff, but his body wasn't too bad, and he had been swimming a lot recently. Kary gave his hairy chest an appreciative once over then nodded at his trousers. Mark released the belt then teasingly undid the buttons one by one.

Kary nibbled the end of a finger as the anticipation got to her. Mark eventually let his chinos drop and stepped out of them. He stood with hands on his hips and raised his eyebrows at Kary. She extended her nibbled finger to point at his boxers, particularly the area which was bulging out. "You drop yours and I'll drop mine. You first."

Mark hooked his thumbs under the waistband of his boxers and slowly pulled them out and down, slowly revealing his erection. Kary kept wagging her finger as he teased her, urging him to take it a little further down each time. She licked her lips when she saw the deep red tip of his cock, and smiled as more and more of the thick shaft was revealed. Eventually the boxers were halfway down Mark's thighs and his hard on was fully on display. Kary nodded approval. Mark whipped the boxers off, tossed them aside and stood proudly displaying himself.

Satisfied Mark had fulfilled his obligation, Kary quickly pushed her knickers down and put them aside. Her flat stomach tapered down to a trimmed triangle of pubic hair which pointed down to plump lips. They each spent a while admiring the other's groin, until Kary asked, "So, how do we use one of those plugs?"

Mark moved to stand in front of Kary so that his hard on pressed against her belly. He ran a finger over her breasts and around her nipples, which were stiff and sensitive. She took his hand and guided it down to her pussy lips, pushing his forefinger into her warm, wet vagina. She made appreciative noises as he pushed it deeper into her. They kissed passionately and she ground her hips against his hand.

When they finally parted, Kary nodded at the bed and said, "So, let's do this. I'm horny as hell."

Mark guided Kary to the bed, a hand cupping each firm round buttock in turn. "Lie down on the bed. On your front."

When she had stretched out, Kary arched her back so her buttocks were raised up and prominent. Crouching between her legs, Mark ran a finger over the curve of each- down from the base of her spine to the tops of her thighs and back again. She liked this, making happy noises into the mattress. Mark ran the fingers of his left hand down the cleft between her buttocks until he reached the puckered ring of her sphincter. He spread her buttocks and the ring of muscle dilated a little. It glistened with the lubricant Kary had already squeezed in.

Mark lined up the smaller butt plug, lubricant and condoms within easy reach. He squeezed lube onto his right index finger and placed it against the entrance to Kary's arse. She squeaked, not just because of the cold liquid against her sphincter, but also with trepidation at what it signalled. Mark pushed his finger into her, and her arse rose up to meet it.

As Mark pumped his finger in and out of her, Kary tensed up, clasping the covers tight. Something warm and beautiful was building deep inside her and she didn't want him to stop. She whimpered when he removed his finger. She squeaked happily when something new- the small butt plug she thought, hoped- nudged at her sphincter.

Mark spread lube over the shaft of the plug as he moved it around the edge of Kary's butt hole. When he was certain it was slippery enough he began pushing it into her. It tapered out along its length, before pinching back in near the base. Every time Mark pushed it in, Kary tensed and pushed it back a little. Centimetre by tantalising centimetre he fed it into her, each time a little further, until she lifted her buttocks up toward the plug and started grinding against it.

With one last push the flare of the plug passed the ring of muscle and popped in. She let out a low, very happy sigh and started rotating her arse so she could feel the plug move in her butt. "So. Good." she managed to purr.

Mark watched the glorious sight of Kary's butt rotating. He sat back and ripped open a condom and rolled it down his rock hard erection. With his left hand he reached under Kary and drew two fingers gently over her skin, one either side of her hot wet pussy lips. Then he pushed the fingers, together, back up, sliding them into her. She buried her head in the pillow. A muffled request, "Fuck me." told him just what he wanted to hear.

Kary lifted her arse higher and Mark shuffled forward and angled his cock into her. The head lodged between the slick lips and she grasped the cushions. "In...." was all she could say. Mark grasped her waist and pulled her to him as he pushed in, inspiring a victorious cry of "Yes!"

With each thrust Mark ground the plug into Kary's arse, raising groans of joy. As orgasm approached she pushed back against him harder and faster. She screamed as she came, shakes and shivers running through her body.

Kary buried her head in the pillow as exquisite sensations turned her to jelly. Mark held still, enjoying the clasping warmth. When she could move again, at least enough to raise her head, Kary announced, "I want you to fuck me in the ass."

Mark grinned. He'd wanted to hear that. He eased out of her and grabbed the lube.

Kary's buttocks rotated as she waited impatiently for Mark's next move. The movement stopped as soon as he grasped the butt plug's base. His fingers slid on the lube coated toy, until he hooked them around it and began to pull it out. She made happy little whimpers as it withdrew and a sad squeak when it popped out. Mark immediately dribbled lube over his cock and presented it to her arse.

Mark pushed into Kary's arse, easing against her sphincter carefully. "Hell, yes!" she called out as the cock head squeezed through the ring of muscle, "Put it there!" She sighed as she tried to relax and let him past, then gasped as he made it.

Kary's sphincter squeezed tight around Mark's shaft and he paused to relish it. Then he pushed slowly and strongly into her, lodging himself gently but firmly in the tight passage. When he was as deep inside Kary as he could go he held himself there, breathing hard and feeling his heart drum in his chest. Grasping her waist tighter he began to pull out again. He halted again as she shivered and gasped with another orgasm.

With all the lube they'd used Mark slid easily in and out of Kary as he built up a rhythm. She was tight around him, drawing the cum out of him with every stroke. Their gasps and grunts were merging as they both pushed on to climax.

Kary came first, letting go a loud, jubilant "YES!!!" She clasped around Mark's cock, pushing him over the edge so he filled the condom deep inside her.

They sank to the bed and slowly slid apart. "Wow." said Kary after a while.

"Wow." echoed Mark.

"Thank you. I've wanted to do that for so long." Kary stretched. "I'm heading for Italy tomorrow."

"Germany for me." Mark admitted, "In a couple of days."

"I don't have to check out until noon. We can do more stuff until then. When I get my energy back."

Don't miss out!

Visit the website below and you can sign up to receive emails whenever Mary Tales publishes a new book. There's no charge and no obligation.

https://books2read.com/r/B-A-XESE-PSQO

BOOKS 2 READ

Connecting independent readers to independent writers.

Also by Mary Tales

Jiggles
Jiggles and the Test Pilot
Jiggles and the Archaeologists
Jiggles and the Flying Boats

Love By The Book
Love By The Book
Love The Weekend

Mary Tales Collections
Mary Tales Omnibus
Contact Adventures
Contact Adventures 2 - First Timers
Cassie Gets it On
The Adventures of Jiggles

Meet The Gang
Meet The Gang

www.ingramcontent.com/pod-product-compliance
Lightning Source LLC
Chambersburg PA
CBHW072010150726
47999CB00002B/583